KAREN AND THE MICRO-BUDDIES:

THE SURFACTANTS

Sally Kuzniewski

PRISTINE
PRESS AND MEDIA

Karen and the Micro-buddies
Copyright © 2024 by Sally Kuzniewski

ISBN
000-0-00000-000-0 (Paperback)
000-0-00000-000-0 (eBook)

Dedication Page

*For our readers for believing in the power
of imagination and the joys of science*

Acknowledgment

I would like to thank Nick Pappas and the team at New Line Cinema for their encouragement to publish this book. Matt Hayward, Reno Smith, and the team at Pristine Press worked tirelessly and dedicatedly. This book would not have been possible without them.

Table of Contents

Chapter 1

The Daily Grind

The coffee swayed in the mug in Karen's hands. She looked all around at her t-shirt for any spills. "Phew," she let out a sigh of relief. She slowed down but walked briskly across the carpeted floor towards the door. *What has Andy got so early in the morning*" she wondered, as she put her coffee on the side table. Her mind ran into the dinner date from last night as she unlatched the door. As she opened it, she was greeted with big red roses in a sparkling vase.

"Good morning. This is for Karen Smith," the delivery guy said as he handed out a signature pad.

"I'm Karen," Karen replied blushingly. The guy smiled at her as she signed the pad.

"Have a good day, Ms. Smith," he said as Karen took the rose bouquet from him.

"Thanks, you too," Karen replied, still blushing and she closed the door.

She quickly looked at the roses to find a card buried in the middle. It said "Good morning sweetie, I enjoyed your company last night ☺ Hope you have a fun day with your micro-buddies.- Andy". As she took the plastic off the roses and put the vase on the coffee table, her mind raced through last night at Grillaconi, the moose Andy drew and the microbuddy Karen drew, the cartoon comic between their drawings, and their laughter over it. They both loved to draw.

A humming sound brought Karen out of the thought and she ran to the bedroom. She picked up the papers strewn on the floor by the printer, added more paper to the printer and pressed the OK button. As the printer resumed printing, Karen hurriedly put the printed pages in order. She looked at one of the figure for the line plot. "Oh well," she said, as she went back to her desktop computer, opened the file, and started working on the figure. The two color lines for the graph were not distinguishable on the black and white printout, although she had made one a darker gray. She corrected this by using different line patterns rather than colors. This was for her weekly work progress which she was going to discuss with her advisor, Dr. Allison Rogers. Karen was just a year into her Masters program at the University of BioResources and Technology and she tremendously enjoyed working with Dr. Rogers. Karen was a diligent worker and she was in love with science. But she was also hard on herself. If she caught her mistakes, she would correct them. That was the quality she loved about herself and she knew that Dr. Rogers liked as well. *There I go*, Karen said to herself as she looked at the printed out figure. She stapled the other stack of printouts, which was a journal paper, also a part of the discussion with Dr. Rogers for that day for future research work.

As Karen walked down the street with her backpack, her thoughts were on the results for the 16S microbial profiling on the ABI, the gene sequencer machine. She was trying to profile the microbial communities in the crude-oil contaminated sediment samples she got from offshore Cape Cod. This she did using the 16S ribosomal DNA-terminal restriction fragment length polymorphism (16S rDNATRFLP) technique. Her positive control was the *Marinobacter* sp. This was commonly found in sediments and thus was used. The negative control was water.

The 16S-rDNA-TRFLP technique

This involved extracting the DNA first, purifying it and then amplifying the 16S region on the DNA using the polymerase chain reaction (PCR) that employs a forward primer and a reverse primer. The forward primer was labeled with a fluorescent tag. The PCR products were then purified and then were digested with restriction enzymes. These enzymes cut the PCR products at specific sites and so this results in different length fragments for different organisms. The differently digested PCR fragments can then be run on capillary electrophoresis on the ABI machine. This will give peak analyses with the tallest peak for the biggest fragment. However, to find what each peak corresponds to, in other words to interpret the TRFLP profile on the ABI, a clone library is created for the restriction enzyme digested PCR products after running them on a polyacrylamide gel electrophoresis. The digested PCR fragments are cloned into a vector and then used for PCR, and then sequenced on the ABI. Both cloning and PCR amplifies the fragments and both are used to give lots of amplified fragments. The sequences are then cleaned and used for phylogenetic analyses on the PAUP™ software, staring with BLAST. The peak corresponds to the length of the fragment and by sequencing the fragment, the identity can be determined by the PAUP™ software.

The sample site was located off the shores of Cape Cod. An oil refinery company, Gooey Oil Refinery, located in the hub of Boston city, regularly transported its crude oil cargo from Cape Cod. Although it never happened, they were concerned about oil spillage in the nearby water and wanted to be prepared for such accidents. They eventually contacted Dr. Rogers at the University of BioResources and Technology to research oil bioremediation in Cape Cod. One of the biggest concerns with oil spills is offshore contamination. The oil, via waves, is washed onto the shores and contaminates the shoreline. It was the shoreline samples from Cape Cod, located near the in-port, that Karen and Dr.

Rogers were working with. All the loading took place at the in-ports. The in-port was also located closer to the city and so it made sense to start the study from that site. They collected offshore sediment samples from there and also samples of crude oil from the cargo ships for Gooey Oil Refinery.

Karen grew up in Honolulu in the breezy, salty air of the beaches. An avid scuba diver, she was protective of the marine creatures. This led her to pursue an undergraduate degree in marine biology. She had seen and heard it all. Algal blooms, polluted water, dying organisms. Her dad chartered boats and she helped him clean these boats. It was around this time that she heard of a shipwreck off the coast of Honolulu. The news flashed on the TV, showing blackishgrey plumes floating on the water and the shores littered with dead, oiled fishes and birds.

"They won't let us go there," said her Dad when Karen, one day while on the boat with him, asked if they could see what was happening.

"Why can't people be more careful in the water? Do they ever impose damage fines on these careless people? she thought. But this one experience made her steely and determined to learn to protect the marine creatures.

Karen majored in Biology at the Manao University of Marine Resources where she took courses in marine biology and microbiology. Her honors project studies the effects of petroleum on fishes and the water. She set her huge salt water fish tank with the water and the fishes from off the coast of Honolulu. Then she maintained the salinity, temperature, dissolved oxygen, and other chemical parameters so as to mimic the natural environmental conditions. When the conditions were stable, she added different concentrations of petroleum to different tanks and then measured its concentrations in the different parts of the tank environment, including in the fishes' tissues at different time points. In this project, Karen learned to use analytical instruments to measure the concentration of the major components of petroleum in her samples. The lighter components evaporated and did not stay for a long time. But the creosote in the petroleum persisted longer in the sediment and prominently led to lesions and reproductive problems in fishes. Mass spectrometry of the samples from the tanks showed that they were composed of HMW-PAHs (high molecular weight polyaromatic hydrocarbons).

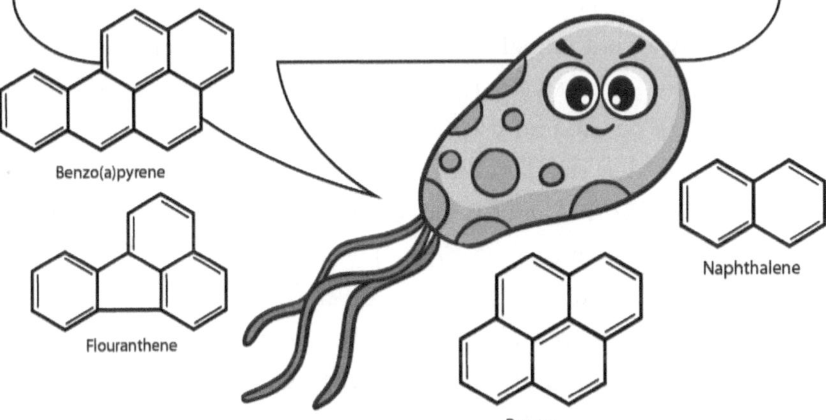

Karen noticed that the LMW-PAHs decreased faster in concentration in the sediment than the HMW-PAHs which mostly stayed in the sediment and also in fish adipose tissues. The fishes developed lesions on their skins and simply died in large numbers. She believed the fishes died because of the HMW-PAHs. Many of the papers she read mentioned that some of the HMW-PAHs such as benzo (a)pyrene are toxic, possibly carcinogenic. She believed that this killed the fishes, although that investigation was not part of her honors project.

John and Erin looked occupied over something on their table as Karen flung in through the door of the Blue Cove Building.

"Hello guys, what's up?" Karen asked as she dived into a chair next to them. John excitedly turned a spreadsheet around to Karen.

"AG-1 stays alive even at 100 mg of chrysene per liter of medium. But it can't survive at that concentration of creosote," John said excitedly. He was referring to a *Rhodococcus* strain AG-1, isolated in Dr. Rogers' lab from the soils of a petroleum refinery site in East Providence, Rhode Island.

"That sucks, doesn't it?" Erin said, chewing rapidly on her candy, and waved the candy pack at Karen.

"Looks fun to me," Karen said as she took a piece of candy from the pack. John Wright and Erin Turner were undergraduate students at the University of Bioresources and Technology. They were doing an honors project in Dr. Rogers' laboratory to investigate the effects of different concentrations of individual PAHs, their mixtures, and creosote on the growth of AG-1. This was part of an attempt to evaluate if AG-1 had the potential to be used for creosote remediation.

Karen looked at the data for the abiotic control. No growth at all. Then she looked at the data for the cellular protein for the triplicates in each experiment. Erin seemed right. The strain was alive in chrysene but was dying as the concentration of creosote increased. For this work, John and Erin grew a pure culture of *Rhodococcus* strain AG-1 in minimal salt medium. This medium contained the vital minerals and salts required for microbial growth. It doesn't have any carbon source. First, the mineral salt medium was prepared in individual flasks. The flasks were sealed with nylon stoppers and autoclaved. To this, they added different concentrations of chrysene or creosote. Chrysene is sold as crystals and as it is difficult to accurately measure tiny concentrations of it on a weight scale, they dissolved a known amount of chrysene in acetone. This was their stock solution. Then, using the concentration-volume equation, they measured how much of the stock solution to add to the medium. This solution was added to the hot medium from the autoclave. This was done to evaporate the acetone which is a carbon source too. The chrysene was left behind as a fog on top of the medium. Flasks to which creosote needed to be added were left to sit for a while to cool off the medium first. Then the flasks were inoculated with a known cellular protein concentration of concentration of AG-1. The inoculum was taken from the mid exponential phase. The abiotic control had everything the other flasks had but were not inoculated. This was done to see any chemical effects on chrysene and creosote. It was also set up to check for contamination arising from the chemical or physical components of the set-ups. Then samples were taken from the flask into clean microfuge tubes to account for data at time zero. The stoppers were put on and the flasks were left in the dark at room temperature and swirling on a shaker at 70 rpm. At selected time intervals, more samples were taken. These were used to estimate the cellular protein concentration using the BioRad™ protein assay. For this, the samples were spun in a centrifuge for 15 minutes at 6000 rpm to separate the cell pellet from the medium. The medium was discarded and in its place, mineral medium without any chrysene or creosote or any other supplement was added. This was vortexed to mix the cells with the medium. The sample was centrifuged and the medium replaced with fresh medium and the whole thing was done once again. The cell pellet mixed with the fresh medium was placed in an icewater bath and sonicated to lyse the cells. This released the cellular protein, the concentration of which was measured on the spectrophotometer using the BioRad protein assay.

"Look at this," Karen said, pointing to the day 17 cellular protein concentration for AG-1, grown on 50 parts per million chrysene. It was 5.1 μg of cellular protein per mL of medium.

"Yep, cool, isn't it?" Erin said.

"We're going to keep going with the experiment. Let's see what happens," said John, as they all gathered their back packs.

"So how was dinner last night?" asked Erin.

"Dinner? Oh…dinner. It went well. We went to Grillaconi," Karen blushed as she continued. "The chicken pot pie was delicious."

"What about the movie?" asked John.

Erin blushed even harder and said, "we didn't go. We came home."

"What about you?" Karen attempted to ask Erin who, along with John, were looking mischievously at her

"Mike and I went to Blue Rock", replied Erin. They talked about their outings for a while and then they all headed to their respective places, John and Erin to their classes and Karen to the lab.

Karen's mind was running over what she needed to do. Meet with Dr. Rogers, check the results from the ABI, then carry on from there for preparing the sequences for BLAST.

"Good morning Jose," Karen said as she stepped out of the elevator.

"Morning," replied Jose with a smile and then continued with the sweeping.

Jose was the janitor there. He was always seen sweeping the floor early mornings, five days a week. A short, skinny and quiet guy, he was always smiling at people who passed by, and also generous. Once, Karen needed a snapshot of herself for an article she had written for a student's magazine. It was early morning and there was no one around on the floor. She saw Jose, who willingly left his mop and snapped a picture of Karen. He kept doing retakes until Karen was satisfied with the snapshots. On another occasion, after he came to know from John about his need for a chair because the old one in the undergraduate students' office broke, he came back that afternoon with a study chair he found in the surplus room.

"Wow, look at that," Dr. Rogers said excitedly as she looked at the two graphs on her desk.

"Yes. Benzo (a)pyrene in the crude oil is degraded 18% by the consortium. But not all of it is significantly degraded when it is used as the sole substrate," Karen explained, as she pointed with her pen tip to the two graphs.

"The abiotic control looks good too, no degradation," added Dr. Rogers.

Karen had been studying the degradation of PAHs that were in the crude oil. She had set-up flasks with diluted crude oil-contaminated sediment that the group collected on the expedition with Dr. Rogers. For her first experiments, she diluted the creosote-contaminated sediment with the seawater. Every week, Karen took out 10mL samples from the flasks. She first centrifuged the samples to separate the cells from the liquid. She did this three times to make sure the cells didn't have much of the chemicals spun with them. She re-suspended the cells in physiological saline which was 0.1% sodium chloride solution. This solution kept the cells viable rather than bursting out, which happens in plain water. She used the cell suspension for measuring the protein concentration in the cells. This was done with the Bradford assay. The concentration of the cells gives a measure of cell density. She used the liquid portion, from centrifugation, for ethyl acetate extraction. This was done to extract all the organic chemicals. The extract was dried over sodium anhydrous sulfate to remove any water that might be in it. Then the extract was placed in a water bath at 50°C. The hot water evaporated the acetone and left behind the PAHs. This was then cooled off and then a chemical called N-Methyl-N- (trimethylsilyl) trifluoroacetamide (MSTFA) was added. This was done to replace the anionic oxygen with methyl groups. This would prevent the PAHs from binding to each other and with other chemicals. This basically allowed the PAHs to be detected by gas chromatography mass spectrometry. They could also be measured on this instrument.

For four months, no changes in the concentrations of the HMW-PAHs were seen but the LMW-PAHs decreased to about 23%. The abiotic control, which had sodium azide to kill off the microbes, showed 11% decrease in the concentration of LMW-PAHs but none for HMW-PAHs. Some of the LMW-PAHs can undergo photolysis or volatilization. The 12% decrease in concentration by the microbes in six months was not significant as these chemicals have been shown to be more rapidly degraded by other studies. The microbial biomass increased very slowly, by up to 7%, and then disappeared by four months, which means that the microbes died. The HMW-PAHs are the main concern when they are in the environment. They do not degrade easily and can be toxic to the environment. So, Karen set up another experiment in which she diluted the creosote-contaminated sediment with a mineral salt medium. As the name implies, this is a medium that contains minerals required for microbial growth. And it worked. The LMWPAH concentrations started changing from day 2 and the cellular protein concentration started increasing. The HMWPAH concentrations started decreasing from day 5.

Dr. Rogers reclined back in her chair and asked, so, what does this tell us?"

"That benzo [a]pyrene can be degraded in the presence of other PAHs. And I think one reason is because the other PAHs can allow the production of aspecific enzymes that can use benzo [a]pyrene as a substrate. Another reason is the higher biomass for the consortia. Which means more bacterial cells, more enzymes to break down benzo [a] pyrene. Umm I think ummm," Karen's eyebrows turned into a furrow. Dr. Rogers kept looking at her, and then she smiled and said, "come on out with it".

"Oh well, I was just thinking that it could be due to biosurfactants production. You know, with more biomass, more biosurfactants production to solubilize the benzo [a]pyrene. Also, there could be PAHs such as catechols that act as surfactants and aid in the solubilization of benzo [a]pyrene."

Dr. Rogers's face lit up but she kept quiet in deep thoughts. "Yes, I agree with you. Now, we can plan on the enzyme assays. Make a list of the oxygenases involved in PAH metabolism and we will go with that. Let's look into biosurfactants later."

"Yes, one step at a time," Karen said happily as Dr. Rogers gave Karen back the graphs. "So how is Millie feeling?" asked Karen as she put the graphs in the fold of her lab notebook.

"Ah, Millie," Dr. Rogers shook her head and let out a giggle. "Millie got well as soon as it was 9 am. She came to me and said, Mommy I think I will play outside to get better." They both laughed. "She spent a few hours playing

outside and then came in and did a painting."

"I hope you were able to get some work done yourself," said Karen.

"I did for a little bit till 12 noon until Millie came inside and then it was on and off between my computer and paying attention to Millie. Here is the painting she did." It had Millie next to her Mom. Her Mom was wearing a crown.

On top of the paper was written, I love you Mommy.

"Cute," said Karen.

"Hm hm" said Dr. Rogers as Karen got up and said, "see you later!"

"Yes" replied Dr. Rogers as Karen left for her office.

Karen loved meeting with Dr. Rogers. She was her role model, that is what she thought. Dr. Allison Rogers was an assistant professor at the Department of Marine Research at the University of BioResources and Technology in Boston. She got her Ph.D. degree from Baltimore University of Marine Sciences in Maryland. Dr. Allison Rogers met her husband, Jason, in high school, and they had a five year old girl, Millie. An easy-going but hard working person, Dr. Allison Rogers was well-liked by students, particularly the women.

Karen entered her lab on the fifth floor in a white lab coat.

The radio in the lab was playing to Anke Melody.

"Hello," said Karen in a sing-song tone.

"Hey", Amy looked up from her bench. She was making microbial culture medium. "I got something to show you," she said, and pulled out a printed article. Karen looked at it, read the title, skimmed over the abstract, and was flipping through the pages.

"Holy shit! They engineered an isolate and had it churnned out butanol!" she exclaimed.

"30mL per liter of medium used," said Amy.

"Imagine butanol produced by microbes. Imagine butanol-run cars, I wonder what they would be like. Maybe like little buggies. Long live the microbes," chuckled Karen. Amy giggled as she swirled the flask and then set it on the stirrer.

"Microbial power," quipped in Amy.

"Thanks for the article," Karen said.

"You're welcome," replied Amy, as Karen walked to her bench. She wiped the bench down with the diluted disinfectant and let it dry while she went to the incubator and brought back a pile of petri plates. She was setting the plates on her bench when Marcus walked in and began singing along to the music. Karen and Amy cheered for him.

"This new album is awesome," said Karen. Amy Walker and Marcus Lopez were Masters students in Dr. Rogers' lab. Amy grew up in Michigan and was working on a project to identify proteins in marine extreme conditions. This was typical of oceans where pressure increases and temperature decreases with increasing height. For this, she was working with samples from the different sites of the Atlantic Ocean.

Marcus grew up in Chicago. His project was on understanding microbial community change in response to carbon loads in local, public spots. For this, he got samples from different nearby beaches.

Dr. Allison Rogers believed that researchers perform well when they are given their own research space with no stepping-on-the-feet involved between people in the same lab. At the same time, she made sure she selected people who were hard-working, outspoken, nice, and can get along with others in the lab. For this, she always had her existing lab members spend a day with a prospective student in the lab. She observed their spontaneous interactions and also had the lab members turn in their evaluation after a few days. That is exactly what happened with Karen, Amy, Marcus, and also with John and Erin before they came into Dr. Rogers' laboratory. When Karen came in, the previous laboratory members consisted of Johanna, Natalie, Mike and Chris. After her interview with Dr. Rogers, Dr. Rogers introduced Karen to them over lunch and she spent the day in the lab with them in a lab coat, helping out with general stuff like helping to make the microbial culture media and pouring the medium into petri plates, or just being around them. Dr. Rogers popped in every now and then, kidding around and to see what they were all up to. Karen was impressed as she had not seen anything like this before. Two days later, Dr. Rogers and the lab group sat in a round table meeting. They handed in their evaluation of Karen to Dr. Rogers, and discussed what they thought. By the end of the meeting, all voted in favor of Karen and Dr. Rogers sent an offer letter to Karen. Over the years, Johanna, Mike, Chris and Natalie all graduated. Johanna and Chris graduated from the Masters program while Mike and Natalie finished off their honors project and graduated from the undergraduate program. Johanna went on to do a Ph.D. at Rochester Institute for Marine Research in NY while Mike also went for a Ph.D. but at Boulder State University in Colorado. Natalie and Chris both went for jobs, with Natalie working for Save the Microorganisms and Chris for AG Mining Research Institute in California. After Karen, Amy came in followed by Erin, Marcus and

John. They all loved Dr. Rogers. She was very caring about their need to do good quality research as well as their future. She would go out of her way to do everything to make sure that her students got to where they wanted in their professional careers. That is exactly what happened with Johanna, Natalie, Mike and Chris. As they proceeded towards the end of the stay in her lab, she made sure that they had all their research work published. When needed, she promptly wrote reference letters, and also provided mock interviews to prepare them for their job and research interviews.

Dr. Allison Rogers' tremendous care for her students' performances and future stemmed from observing her father Dr. Pat Wright, also a professor, and her experience with her own Ph.D. advisor. Dr. Pat Wright was a laid back person. "A happy lab is a healthy lab," is what he used to say. Allison's interest in microbiology stemmed from him as she marveled at the work being done in his own lab. It took Allison several bad experiences with advisors before she landed up with Dr. Bob Sorrenson at the Baltimore University of Marine Sciences. First, she attended Chicago Institute of Technology in Illinois for her Ph.D. Her advisor was a very cold and demanding person. Allison was married by then and she did work hard, but could not live up to the lofty expectations even after ten hours of being in the lab every day. She was a research assistant and that took up most of her time, leaving very little time for her own research. She hardly saw her own advisor and every time she went to see him, he was on the phone or not in his office. She was bossed around by her advisor's "favorites". The lab was more of a competing ground than for research. Finally, one day her advisor called her in the office and suggested that she leave the program with the reasons, "you didn't do all the work I expected you to do." Allison stood in front of him, with tears rolling down her cheeks. Luckily, her comfort was her own parents and Jason. She worked for a while until Jason got a lucrative job offer in Maryland. That's when she thought of doing a Ph.D. Dr. Bob Sorrenson was a caring, dedicated advisor and Allison's role model. She learned how to manage her own lab from her wonderful time under his guidance and then as a postdoctoral fellow at Marine Sciences University of Maryland in Dr. George Wilkinson's lab, a long-time colleague of Dr. Sorrenson.

Karen spent the whole day cleaning up the sequences and running them on the PAUP™ software. It was quarter past eight when Karen left Blue Cove building. She was recounting her day in the lab, what she did. She was in the habit of doing it every night as she walked home. There were several occasions when the recount would make her realize that she forgot something in her experimental work. Like that one time when she realized, while recounting, that she had forgotten to check the temperature on the incubator-shaker. The shaker had a lid and the temperature inside it could be adjusted. Karen used the incubator-shaker for keeping her flasks that needed constant stirring. Of course, she made a Uturn. It turned out that the temperature was set at room temperature, exactly what Karen needed. But it wasn't always this easy. Like this one time when she forgot to add the yeast extract in her microbial growth medium. She went back, impatient to dig into her lab notebook to find out how she made that horrible mistake. It was written right there. Karen writes the method fully in her lab notebook. As soon as Karen is done following a step, she ticks it off in her lab notebook. This time, the addition of yeast extract was not ticked. Karen made the yeast extract solution and the wait seemed to take forever as it was being autoclaved. Then it had to cool down before she can handle it to add it to the microbial growth medium. Meanwhile, she went in for a quick snack, munching and sat down to calculate how much of the stock yeast solution to add in her microbial growth medium. She used the volume-concentration formula. She had her cell phone off on these occasions so that she could concentrate fully on her work. Of course, when she got home there were messages waiting on her answering machine, most of them from Andy, her Mom, her Dad, again and again. And she spent a lot of such nights comforting her parents while poor Andy put together a dinner for her. But she is not lucky all the time to not let the whole work get wasted. Like this one time when she had set up PCR in the thermocycler. She was recounting her day when it occurred to her that she was supposed to use the concentrated Taq and not the diluted one. She couldn't find any concentrated Taq and had asked Dorothy from the neighboring lab if she could borrow from her. Dorothy agreed with, "just a few minutes" but never got back and meanwhile Karen got started on her PCR, forgot all about it, and added the diluted Taq sitting in her microfuge tube rack. Of course, it was all ruined. She didn't bother to go back and set up another PCR as that would take 45 minutes for her and she was tired. She redid the whole thing the next day but had to wait half a day to get hold of the concentrated Taq from Dorothy, who apparently was extremely busy.

This time, it all went well. No mistake in her work that day. Karen got home and the first thing she did was to call Andy. He had been busy with his security guard job and taking courses at night for an Associate degree in criminology. He was just out of class that evening when Karen called him and was heading home for dinner. Karen washed her hands and quickly changed into her fresh gym clothes. She hurriedly set the pasta to boil and took a bag of cut up broccoli and grilled turkey from the freezer when Andy walked in.

"We are having grilled turkey with broccoli and pasta," said Karen.

"That sounds nice," said Andy as he sank onto the couch.

Every Sunday, she would clean and cut up all the veggies she had bought on Saturday and vacuum-seal them and put them in the freezer. She would also grill turkey or chicken and cut them up and refrigerate them. It allowed her to have a good meal during the week when she often stayed up late with her work. She would alternate the days between turkey or chicken and sometimes fish, steak or pork.

Both Andy and Karen were fitness freaks. They would work out every alternate day in the gym for about an hour.

"Ready for the gym?" Karen asked as she came out of the kitchen.

"Yeah," replied Andy as he gave her a kiss and picked up his gym bag.

Karen had always been a fitness freak. Her mother worked as a school teacher but managed to cook every day for the family. Karen developed her love for cooking from her mother. Karen and Andy met one and a half years ago while training for the triathlon in Boston. They started going out for coffee and then for dinner dates. Eventually, they moved in together. Their parents met last

Christmas and Karen's mother had been nagging her if he had yet proposed. Karen felt that he might and if he did, she would accept it. She was completely in love with this tall, handsome, and of course very kind guy. But as of now, her focus was on her Masters degree and enjoying the tranquility of the relationship.

They watched TV after dinner every week day and then Andy would study while Karen would get on her computer for a couple of hours to continue with her writing, or sit on her desk to read a paper, or sometimes would bring over her lab notebook to update it, write in it, or to do data analyses. Tonight, she was continuing with the review manuscript on creosote contamination and remedial strategies. She would usually stay up till 1am in the morning and get up by 9am the next day. No exception or she would feel grouchy the whole day and wouldn't get anything done. She needed her eight hours of sleep. On the weekends, she usually spent Saturday mornings getting stuff done either in the lab or at her desk, and then took off for the rest of the weekend with Andy. In the summer, they would go to the beach or hiking. In the winter, they would rent movies or play video games. They visited family occasionally. Last Easter, Karen had joined Andy for his family get-together in Florida.

Karen finished doing a table on bacterial communities known to degrade creosote. She went through the paper stack that she used to make the table to make sure they were in the table and were referenced. Then she made a note on her to do list to briefly describe the table in the text. Next, she made another note on her list to find more papers to compare the different remedial options for creosote. She looked up at the wall clock. 1:09 am. She saved her document, and turned off the computer. A while later, she dozed off into a deep sleep.

Chapter 2

The Magic Rub

Karen looked at the results on the screen for the bacterial identification work she did using the 16S rDNA-TRFLP technique. She used samples from the crude oil-contaminated shore of Cape Cod. These samples were used in her experiment too on crude oil degradation. She sequenced the 16S rRNA from the subsamples right after sampling at the site and also at selected time-points including at time-zero from her experiment. She graphed the abundance.

"*Mycobacterium vanbaleenii* strain AP1, *Sphingomonas paucimobolis* strain EPA 505, *Rhodococcus* sp. UW1, *Pseudomonas stutzeri* strain G1, *Bacillus subtilis*, *Thalassolitius oleivorans* gen. nov., *Oceanospirillum* sp., *Alcanivorax burkumensis* strain SK 2T." Karen read off the results for the blast search for her sequences for the samples right from the sampling site. The results were identical to those for the samples at time zero for her experiment. She looked at the results on her graph for the later time points from her experiment and realized that the abundance of some of the microbes decreased. *Sphingomonas paucimobilis* strain EPA 505 was not detected from day 15. *Rhodococcus* sp. UW1, *Bacillus subtilis*, and *Pseudomonas stutzeri* strain G1 slowly decreased in abundance. From 28 days, they accounted for just 21% of the total abundance. *Thalassolitius oleivorans* gen. nov., *Oceanospirillum* sp., *Alcanivorax burkumensis* strain SK 2T, and *Mycobacterium vanbaleenii* AP1 dominated over all others starting from 28 days in the experiment.

She looked at the controls. The positive control was an isolated *Oceanospirillum* sp., strain AS1. *Oceanospirillum* sp. Strain AS1 commonly occurred in the seawater and so it was used as the positive control. The negative control was water. These were also used for the PCR and showed up as single bands of the right size, indicating no contamination along the way when the techniques were carried out. Karen looked at the sequences for these. Good. Nothing for the water control. She then checked to see if the sequence for the positive control would match for *Oceanospirillum* sp. Strain AS1. The BLAST results pointed out to it being 100% *Oceanospirillum* sp. Strain AS1. So the quality control was good for the sequencing.

Survival of the fittest, Karen said to herself as her mind wandered into the reasons for the results. She knew that *Alcanivorax burkumensis* strain SK 2T produced sugar surfactants. Some microbially produced surfactants that can harm other microbes. For example, can the sugar surfactant produced *by Alcanivorax burkumensis* strain SK 2T be killing the other microbial strains except *Thalassolitius oleivorans* gen nov., *Oceanospirillum* sp., and *Mycobacterium vanbaleenii* AP1? Maybe it killed *Sphingomonas paucimobolis* strain EPA 505 totally or to such low abundance that it cannot be detected any longer? Why are *Thalassolitius oleivorans* gen nov., *Oceanospirillum* sp., and *Mycobacterium vanbaleenii* AP1 there? Maybe they also utilize the sugar surfactant produced by *Alcanivorax burkumensis* strain SK 2T to solubilize the hydrophobic PAHs from the crude oil for carbon and energy sources. Or maybe they also produce their own surfactants to aid in this metabolism. This made better sense, or else there would be competition and *Thalassolitius oleivorans* gen nov., *Oceanospirillum* sp., and *Mycobacterium vanbaleeniii* would not be found in significantly similar abundance as *Alcanivorax burkumensis.*

Karen thought about pathways and what it meant for the results she looked at. No *Sphingomonas paucimobolis* strain EPA 505 from day 15. *Rhodococcus* sp. UW1, *Bacillus subtilis,* and *Pseudomonas stutzeri* strain G1 decreased in abundance over time. *Thalassolitius oleivorans, Oceanospirillum* sp., *Alcanivorax burkumensis,* and *Mycobacterium vanbaleeniii* strain AP1 dominated from day 28. So beside the surfactants, it could be that the intermediates or products formed from crude oil metabolism by each of the members or by all the members from day

28 killed or rendered below detection the abundance of *Sphingomonas paucimobolis* strain EPA 505 and decreased the abundance of the others. Are there different pathways occurring by different organisms here or are they the same? Got to be different pathways. Why will an organism carry out a metabolic pathway only to have itself killed in the process? Doesn't usually happen in nature. Karen thought about limited resources in the experiment. Nutrients, iron, carbon and energy sources. Maybe some of these or all got limited and *Sphingomonas paucimobilis* strain EPA 505 didn't have a way to get them while *Rhodococcus* sp. UW1, *Bacillus subtilis*, and *Pseudomonas stutzeri* strain G1 "struggled to get them" and the others found a way to get the required resources and were able to dominate the scene.

Her thoughts kept running while she touched one of the experimental flasks sitting on her lab bench. It had the blackish-looking sediment slurry in it. She rubbed the flask with the palm of her right hand as if feeling sorry for the microbes, all the while thinking about what must be going on to explain the results on abundance. She felt sorry for the flask. She imagined that it was like a pet dog unable to tell her in language about its feelings or needs. And she stroked the flask with her right palm downward. One, two, three times.

Suddenly, she felt being sucked in. It felt like being sucked by a vacuum cleaner. Rrrrrrrrrrrrrrrr. Her hair, her lab-coat, her jeans, her shoes, all were being sucked into something. She could feel her skin being sucked in. It was like putting a vacuum cleaner on your hands. That feel. It was all over her. There was black darkness all around.

In a vacuum cleaner? Karen thought to herself. She wasn't near a vacuum cleaner. She didn't even see one. She had been sitting on a chair in the lab. She remembered the chair she was sitting on. It was a blue chair with leathery, soft covering. The bottom was round and was comfortably soft when she sat on it. The chair had a back support. And it had long legs that were silver and cold to the touch. She could adjust the height of the chair. She had been thinking about her work. There had been no vacuum cleaner around.

What is going on? Where am I going? Karen thought to herself. Suddenly, she was scared. She stretched out her hands and feet to get a grip of something. There was nothing, just pure blackness all around her. And she was being sucked in.

"Help!" Karen yelled. "Help me! Help!!" and then yelled as loud as she could and her throat felt itchy and she gave out a few coughs. She was being sucked in.

Where am I going? Karen wondered, as she thought about stuff going down in a vacuum cleaner. Karen didn't really know how a vacuum cleaner worked. But she could imagine. Through the long pipes. What about going though the filter? Won't she be stuck on it? And she thought that if she was, she would be stuck on the filter. The sucking air would suck and suck at her skin until it tore apart and then the little debris and blood will go through the filter. What if there is a motor, something narrow, and sharp or both along the way?

Unless of course, the vacuum cleaner turns off. Can some vacuum cleaners turn off by themselves if something is stuck anywhere in them? Or maybe, by luck, someone will turn it off. Or maybe, there is someone who sucked her in the vacuum cleaner. Who? She thought about people who possibly would want to do that. Jose? What did she do it him that would make him suck her into a vacuum cleaner? Was he attracted to her and she didn't return the feeling? Was he expecting her to flirt with her or at least be friendly to her? Could it be anyone from the lab? Maybe Andy or Erin or both did it for fun? Or someone felt jealous of her and sucked her in the vacuum cleaner. Amy? Marcus? Yeah, her research was going well and she had started writing papers. And yeah, she got along pretty well with Dr. Rogers. Dr. Rogers? Why would she do that to Karen? Never know. Maybe she really didn't like Karen and what she showed was fake. Maybe she wanted to get rid of Karen because she worked hard in the lab. But she was conservative with the expenses for the lab supplies. Or maybe Dr. Rogers didn't want Karen to succeed. Why would Andy do something like this to her? For fun, to show his skills in criminology? Maybe he had a dark side in him, maybe a psychotic killer side. They had been together for two years and she has not seen anything like this in him. But why get rid of her? Maybe he didn't love her and maybe he was frustrated by the long hours Karen spent on her research work in the lab and at home. And he thought it would be a befitting way for some fun or maybe to kill her. Paternal aunt Sophie? She didn't like Karen or her Mom.

Would she stop being sucked? What if she didn't and she was ripped into pieces? Karen stretched out her hands and feet again in a bid to get a grip of something. Nothing around her.

"Help!!!!!!!!" she yelled as loud as she could, her throat itchy again, and she coughed. She kept yelling and she was being sucked forward into the pure blackness.

Suddenly, she was no longer being sucked. It was deadly still around her in the pure blackness. Karen felt dizzy. She reached out one more time to find something to get a grip on. She stretched out her hands and feet as much as she could. There was nothing. Not even a ground. Was she in zero gravity? She tried jumping. She did go up but then came down. No ground around her. Ok, so there was gravity. Oh yeah, what about the air and the temperature? She took a deep breath. She could breathe but she felt suffocated. And it was stinky like poop. *This has got to be oxygen or I won't live*, she thought. *Maybe there is not much of it.* She felt chilly. *It is cold here. What if it is not regular air, what if it has more nitrogen than 78%? Or maybe the oxygen is mixed with another gas, also poisonous like nitrogen?* Suddenly, that thought scared her. She had to get out of wherever she was in. She started jumping. Didn't help. She went up and then came down into nowhere. She tried scrambling around. Nothing around her to take a grip on. How long would she be in this? What if the air killed her? What if there was a monster lurking around somewhere? She couldn't see, it was pitch dark.

"Help!!!!!!" she yelled. Her throat itched from the yelling. She scrambled around as crazily as she could. She had to get the hell out of here.

Karen felt something moving against her legs. She looked down. It was rod-shaped and tan colored. She kneeled down to look at it carefully. It disappeared in a flash. What was it? A fish? She felt something move against her legs again. She looked down. She saw it again. Rod-shaped and tan. It had little brushes all over its rod-shaped body and one big tail coming out from one end. Or was it something else? It looked like a tail, Karen thought. If she moved, it might disappear.

A fish? Was she in water? Where WAS the water? Karen waved her hands. Then she felt her fingers on her hair. It was all wet, actually swampy. So, was she in a swamp? *No!* She thought to herself. But wait a minute. She took a deep breath, in and then out. She was able to breathe. *How can you breathe in a swamp?* Karen thought. She had to get out of whatever she was in.

What was that? Karen thought and then stood still and looked carefully. There was one tail that kept wobbling against her legs. Karen wanted to grab it. Slowly, she opened her hands wide and made sure she was breathing in and out. She moved her right hand swiftly and grabbed the long tail. Whooooosh! It was moving so fast. Karen put her left hand on it to get a proper grip. She could feel the air pressing against her skin. It was like riding on a speeding motorbike without the helmet and of course, just grabbing the motorbike by its handle without sitting on it. The tail she was holding flapped wildly. Left, right, left, right. And Karen went along with it, left, right, left, right. Then it slowed down. And all around her were a lot more rod-shaped and tan-color creatures. They all looked alike except for the size. They surrounded her. What were they? Unidentified flying objects? Can't be fishes, they didn't look like one. They were all around her. No eyes, no facial features. Just rod-shaped and tanned, each one with one long tail. Could they speak? Would they attack her?

She took a deep breath. *Will they run away? Or will they attack me by probably folding their one tails around me until I suffocate?* Or maybe she would be killed by tail lashing. Ok, she got to test. She let go of the tail. Her heart started pounding. She was drifting again in nowhere. She stretched out her hands and feet. Nothing to grip. Except the tails of these creatures swimming all around her. They were all around her. Suddenly, one swooshed by her back. Then another one by her right leg. Her left leg. Her face. Karen's heart was pounding. Would they attack her? Another one went by her arm. It felt slimy. What were they? They were all around her, swooshing past her body. It felt slimy against her skin.

"No!!!!!!" Karen yelled. She was scared. Her heart was pounding.

Suddenly, they stopped moving. Karen heard a "hi." Couldn't be.

"Hi," she heard it again. *Who's talking?*, she thought and tried to listen carefully But her heart was pounding loudly.

"Hi." She heard it again. Who was it?

"Who is it?" Karen said in a weak voice. A rod-shaped, tanned creature zoomed in her face and said, "Hello, Karen. It is meeeee", and rubbed against her face with its long tail. She wiped off the slime from her face. She was scared out of her wits.

"Help," she yelled and tried running. She tried moving her feet as if she was running. But she felt light-weight and couldn't feel her feet on a solid surface. She couldn't see anything in the pitch darkness except for the rod-shaped, tan creatures. They were all around her and flapped their tails, left and right, left and right. Karen kept trying to run.

"Help me," Karen yelled and kept trying to run. Would she be able to get somewhere? Karen tried running again and the rod-shaped, tanned creatures flapped their tails left and right, right and left. She tried moving her legs faster but didn't feel a solid surface under her feet. And the tails around her flapped faster. Her legs moved still faster and the tails flapped still faster. They were all around her.

Karen kept moving her legs as fast as she could with the hope that maybe she could get out of whatever she was in. And the creatures flapped their tails faster too. They were still all around her. Karen felt exhausted and out of breath. She felt like fainting.

Ok, just relax. This won't get me anywhere, Karen said to herself. She stopped moving her legs and tried breathing in and out, long, slow breaths.

"Relax," she heard the same voice again. It was a manly voice, the same voice that said hi to her before.

"Relax," it said again. It seemed to be coming from in front of her. And in front of here, there was this rod-shaped, tanned creature with a long flapping tail.

"Don't be scared, just relax," the voice said.

"Who is it?" Karen asked weakly.

"It is me, see, I flap my tail," the voice said and the rodshaped, tanned creature in front of her flapped its long tail. Then it flapped its tail harder. "How do you like it?" it asked Karen. "Left, right, left, right," it said. "I put the tail in your face," and it glided the tail against Karen's face.

"Ugh," Karen wiped the slime from her face.

"Ha ha ha. Sorrrrry, I am slimy," it said.

"Ha ha ha ha, wooooow," came group laughter from all around her. And then it came back right in front of her face.

"I am here, in front of you," it said.

"You mean, you are talking?" Karen said, looking at it.

"Yeah, it's me talking, right in front of you. The rodshaped, tanned bacterium," it replied. "Feel me anywhere. Here, I move close to you," it said and it moved closer to Karen. It was stinky.

"Ewww, move," Karen said and it moved away from her face. Karen looked all around her. There were many of them.

The same looking, rod-shaped and tan, each with a tail on one end. The only difference being the size, some were small and some were big but nothing as big as Karen's face. The one in front of her was the biggest she had seen so far. Karen kept looking all around her at the creatures. She had calmed down and her breathing was not rapid anymore. Then she turned to the one on front of her face, the biggest one, and reached out with a finger. She touched the edge of its rod shape. It felt like glue.

"Eew, what is that?" Karen asked as she rubbed her fingers on her pants.

"Slime, my dear. Slime", the voice said, coming from in front of her.

"Ok, let me get this straight. Are you talking?" she said, pointing to the creature in front of her. It wrapped its tail around her arms.

"Yeah, it's me, my tail's around your beautiful arms," the manly voice said.

"Ok, let me make sure. If it is you, the creature with the tail around my arms, can you please take your tail off me?" Karen said. And the tail brushed off her arms.

"Sorrry," it said.

Karen looked at it with curiosity. "How do I know it is you talking?"

"Meeeee…..meeeeee…..meeeee", it said. "Look at my body carefully, Karen. Meeeee meeeeee…" Karen was stunned that it knew her name. She kept looking at it carefully while the sound came.

"Say it again…what's my name?" Karen asked, while looking very carefully at it.

"Karen….sweet Karen," it said in the same manly voice. "Uaaaa ha ha ha ha," it let out a hearty laugh as it brushed its tail against Karen's nose.

"Ugh…. will you stop it…uh…?" Karen said. The tail quickly swooshed past by Karen's face and the bacterium stopped in front of Karen. "How do you know my name?" Karen asked.

"I have seen you grow us," it replied. "Uh, grow you?"

"Yeah, we have seen you grow us in the flasks in your lab," it said. By now, Karen was convinced that she had been whisked in a culture flask. She was WITH the bacteria she grew in her lab. She felt funny. A single tail on a tanned and rod-shaped body….what could it be? There were so many of these around her. And she was working with the culture flask from a contaminated soil area.

Karen remembered the molecular profiling that she did on that culture. *Thalassolitius, Oceanospirillum, Alcanivorax, Mycobacterium* were dominant at the last time she analyzed the flask, i.e. a few days ago. The rod-shaped, tanned bacteria with the long tail kept swirling around her. Karen started remembering the different strains she isolated from the flask and identified using their DNA. She looked at the bacteria moving in a swirly motion around her.

"What are you looking at?" the rod-shaped bacterium said to Karen and swept past her face.

"Nothing…. do you have a name?" Karen asked. By now, she found its behavior cute and wasn't bothered by it sweeping passed her face. Maybe it was playing with her.

"Buddy," it said.

"Buddy, uh?" That was not the response she was looking for. "I mean, do you have a scientific name?" Karen asked.

"What the hell is a scientific name?" the bacterium said. "You, Karen, me Buddy. Karen… Buddy… Karen… Buddy…" it kept lashing the same tail on Karen's nose.

"Alright, I got it, Buddy," Karen said, hoping that it would stop lashing its tail in her nose. It was quite stinky, smelled like soil.

"Good… now, you didn't answer my questions. What is a scientific name?" it asked. "Answer my question, woman," it said and Karen could see its tail propelling forward.

"Will you please stop rubbing your tail on my face?" Karen asked, looking quite irritated.

"Ha ha ha!!! Stinky, huh?" Buddy said and then stopped in front of Karen. There were a lot of other bacteria of different sizes that were identical to Buddy and they were all around Karen. But not lashing in her face or rubbing against her anymore. They didn't bother her. They just drifted all over. In front, in the back.

"So, what is a scientific name?" Buddy asked. It wouldn't let go of the question.

"You won't let that go, will you?" Karen asked.

"Nope," it replied and then started swirling around Karen. "You are stubborn, aren't you?" Karen asked.

"I AM!," it replied in a cute, assertive voice and then swept its tail on Karen's nose and then chortled "ha ha ha ha!" Karen was quite irritated.

"Alright….alright," Karen said and Buddy was again in front of Karen. Its tail was in front of it and it reminded Karen of a dog, a submissive dog sitting in front of the boss. "A scientific name is a name we give to living organisms in science. It has two parts, a genus and a species name. It is used to organize and classify living organisms," Karen explained.

"So what is my genus and species name?" asked Buddy.

"I am not really sure…um…" Karen thought. "Don't know," she finally said. "But as you said, you are a bacterium and you do look like one. Your tail is a flagellum and you are rod-shaped and tan in color. You smell of soil and there are so many of you around."

"Hm hm," said Buddy. "So my tail is called a flagellum. That's a cool word. You know, flagellum like a flag. A flag that waves back and forth. Cool," Buddy said cheerfully as he glided in front of Karen and then stopped. "So my scientific name is Bacteria something?" asked Buddy.

"No, a bacterium is the kingdom you belong to," Karen replied.

"Wait a minute. A kingdom? I belong to a kingdom? Wow!" it said excitedly. "Then that means there must be a king, a queen, some princes and princesses, knights, paupers…" it continued on excitedly before Karen interrupted.

"No, no… not a real kingdom."

"Then what kingdom are you talking about?" Buddy asked, feeling frustrated.

"Kingdom as in science for scientific names. A kingdom is the highest level for classification of living things. There are six kingdoms in science. Kingdom Bacteria, kingdom Archaea, kingdom Protista, kingdom Fungi, Kingdom Plantae, and kingdom Animalia," Karen explained.

"Oh…ok…so I belong to Kingdom Bacteria….and then I have a genus and species name," Buddy said.

"Well, no…after kingdom comes phylum, then class, order, family, genus and then species."

"So what are my names for the others?" Buddy asked, still sitting in front of Karen with its tail in front of it, tapping lightly. Karen knew by now that Buddy asked a lot of questions, that it was stubborn, and if it was not satisfied with the answers, it would sweep its soily-smelling tail on Karen's nose.

"Um…" Karen thought helplessly.

"So you still don't know what is my genus and species?" Buddy asked.

"Nope," Karen replied.

And then, there it goes. Buddy tail's brushed on Karen's nose.

"Ughhh!!!! Stop it, will you?" Karen exclaimed, while trying to rub the tickling feeling and stinkly smell from her nose.

"Wait a minute, you grew us. How come you don't know?" Buddy asked, now with its rod-shaped body in front of Karen's face.

"I did grow you, yes," Karen said. "But I am not sure what you are," she added.

"What does that mean?" Buddy asked. "You did not make me a mutant bacterium, did you?" Buddy retorted, while moving its body close in Karen's face.

"No, no, no," Karen said, nodding her head sideways. She hadn't created mutants from her work yet.

"Then what?" Buddy asked.

"Ok, I did isolate you on nutrient agar plates and I did biochemical tests. And I did come up with a name…" Karen was explaining when Buddy interrupted.

"What's the name?" Buddy asked excitedly.

"Don't know," Karen said. Buddy got away from Karen's face and got in front of her feet, in the same position as it was before with its tail in front of it. Just like a dog.

Karen started to feel guilty. So here she was in a flask full of bacteria that were as big as her. Buddy had given her a ride on its flagellum and it was talking to her. Yes, talking to her. How exciting to have a bacterium talk to you. It just wanted its name and Karen didn't know the name despite growing it. *That's not right,* Karen thought. She tried thinking hard about the isolates she got. " *Thalassolitius, Oceanospirillum, Alcanivorax, Mycobacterium were dominant.* But *Rhodococcus, Bacillus,* and *Pseudomonas accounted for just 21%…* wait a minute… *Pseudomonas??*" Karen thought. Rod-shaped, tan, BUT a single flagellum and it seemed to fit the description of a Pseudomonas as far as Karen knew. However, *Pseudomonas* was not dominant… just accounted for in the 21% and yet, Buddy and its look-alikes were closest in appearance to *Pseudomonas.* Then she remembered she is in the flask and the micro-view is now the macro-view..and wahtever she cannot see due to lack of abundance using human technology, she can now see here. So even though she might not find much of the *Pseudomonas* in her results, she can see a lot of them here in the flask. And Buddy and its look-alikes around her here have the typical physical features of a *Pseudomonas.*

"Buddy, I think your genus name is *Pseudomonas* BUT I am not sure," Karen said excitedly. Buddy looked excited.

"*Pseudomonas,* cool name." "*Pseudomonas,*

Pseudomonas," Buddy kept repeating while circling around Karen with its tail lashing excitedly. Then it stopped. "Why are you not sure?" Buddy asked with one of its long tails at Karen's feet.

"Well, I need to check. I told you that you MIGHT be a Pseudomonas BUT I am not sure," Karen answered and was interrupted by Buddy.

"Why???" Buddy asked and moved its body in different directions as if looking for something and its tail flapped. It was a cute sight. Karen laughed.. "What's funny, woman?" Buddy said.

"Nothing," replied Karen.

"Then what do you need to check?" it asked.

"I need to make sure that what I think is what you are. Science tests," she explained.

"Oh!" It sounded excited and then said, "so what is my species name?"

"You look like *Pseudomonas stutzeri,*" Karen replied.

"Pseudomonas stutter… that is a cool name. Yeah, I like that. I am like Pseudomonas stutter," it said, swimming around Karen. Buddy brushed its tail onto Karen's nose.

"Ewww…. will you please stop that?" Karen was irritated by now.

"Oh, you don't like it?" it asked and then got into Karen face and said,"what do I smell like?" and then moved away. Karen rubbed her nose off with her hands but the soily smell was still there and it didn't help.

"Soil," Karen replied.

"That's not bad, it is?" Buddy asked.

"Uh? I don't know…. No, no… I don't think it is bad for a bacterium," Karen replied.

"Got it…just like the last and the first name of a person, right?" Buddy asked after Karen explained what genus and species means. Its rod-shaped, tanned body was resting at Karen's feet.

"Um…. not really that," Karen replied in deep thought.

"Then what?" Buddy asked, feeling restless.

"Ummm…" Karen felt weird relating family names to scientific names but that was because she never thought of it this way. "Ok, you can think of it this way, I guess. I could be called Karen or Ms. Smith but genealogically, people will want to know what family I belong to.

That is Smith and then who in the Smith family I am which is Karen." Karen explained.

"Hmm," said Buddy and then, "so your genus and species name is Karen Smith?" Buddy asked.

"No, no, no…." Karen replied.

"Then what?" Buddy asked, moving around, and Karen thought it would brush its tail once more in her nose and she quickly replied, "*Homo sapiens.*"

"*Homo sapiens*? What is that?" Buddy asked.

"*Homo* is the genus name for human beings and *sapiens* is the species name."

"Then what the hell is Karen Smith?" Buddy asked and brushed its tail, again on Karen's nose.

"Ewwww…will you stop that?" Karen said.

"Never…fun to have a tail," Buddy said.

"Fun to have hands," Karen replied and tried reaching it with her hands, but Buddy moved so fast and it was impossible for Karen to catch its body or flagellum.

"Ha ha ha…my tail is faster than your two hands," Buddy said.

"Oh well," Karen said.

"Doesn't it tickle you? Doesn't it? Admit it does, I see it on your face. Now answer my questions," Buddy said. Karen realized then that it did tickle her but she was annoyed about the soily smell. But after all, it was a bacterium and that too, from the soil. Then why did it bother her? She had smelled that smell in the lab before when she worked with microbial cultures. Some even had a very pungent smell. Maybe it bothered her here because she probably had highly sensitized senses due to the pit-dark, infinite space around her and seeing live microorganisms around her. Buddy's tail-lashing felt ticklish. "Yeah, it feels ticklish," Karen said.

Buddy said, "Yoohooo, I am good, Karen. I am a good Pseudomonas buddy." And that made Karen laugh. "Me and you…friends," Buddy said, lashing its tail on Karen's head and then rubbing its body on her. Karen laughed. The sight of Buddy doing it was funny. "Friends. So, what is Karen Smith?" Buddy asked.

"It is a name. Just a common name. Karen Smith." Karen explained.

"Got it. Just like *Pseudomonas* Buddy," Buddy said.

"Oh well, *Pseudomonas* is a scientific genus name," Karen explained.

"Ok, how about Buddy uh….," Buddy said. "Buddy Longtail! How's that for MY common name?"

Karen laughed. Buddy was so funny and also smart. By now, she didn't mind its tail lashing or rubbing on her nose. It made Buddy appear cute.

"That sounds good. Buddy Longtail." Karen replied.

"But you will find out my scientific species name, will you and let me know?" Buddy asked.

"Yep, I will," Karen said, as she wondered if she could ever get back in the flask again. "Only if I can come back," Karen said.

"What do you mean by that?" Buddy said, and started swirling around in Karen's face.

"I don't know how I got in," Karen said.

"What????You don't know how you got in?" Buddy asked. "You are kidding me…don't you know what you were doing before you got in here?" Buddy asked, sounding mad. "What were you doing before you came in here?" Buddy asked.

"I was going to take a sample from the flask," Karen answered.

"And then?" Buddy asked. Karen didn't remember.

"I don't know," she replied.

"What do you mean you don't know?" Buddy asked.

"Will you stop asking me tons of questions," Karen snapped at Buddy. Buddy stopped swirling and rested its body at Karen's feet. "All I know was that I was whisked into the flask," Karen said, looking at Buddy. "But I thought you could see what I do. So now, you answer me. How do you think I got into the flask?" Karen asked.

"Won't tell. You won't tell me my species name. Why should I tell what you did to get into my world?" said Buddy. Karen was stunned at the answer.

"Look Buddy, I just don't know your species name right now but I will find out from my lab data and let you know. I promise. I would like to come back. And for that, I would like to know what I did to come in," Karen explained.

"You would?" Buddy asked.

"Of course…it is so much fun working with bacteria. You guys are so fascinating. You guys are everywhere and there is so much more you can do to help the world than what we know," Karen said. Buddy started swirling around Karen's face.

By now, Karen was familiar with Buddy's behavior.

When it was happy and excited, it would swirl around her face. When it was naughty, it would lash its flagellum or brush it on her nose but of course, cutely. And when it was feeling relaxed and wanted to listen to her, it would be at Karen's feet with its flagellum around it.

They were gliding in the flask with Karen holding onto Buddy's flagellum. She saw different forms of microorganisms around her. She saw shiny ones with lots of flagella on one end, she saw yellow tanned ones. She kept gazing at them. Buddy stopped moving.

"Are you going to hold on to me tight and let me take you to the edge of the flask or do you want to stay here?" Buddy asked, looking irritated.

"What? I am just looking. I thought at first that your kind were the only ones around. But now, I see lots of different shapes which tells me that there are others beside your kind," Karen said.

"You thought my kind was the only one here?" Buddy said. "That's stupid, Karen. I thought you knew that there was more than me here. Much more than me…or maybe I am the apple of your eyes and you see nothing beyond me," said Buddy, in a softened voice. It had stop moving and its body was now resting at Karen's feet, with Karen still holding onto its flagellum.

"Oh yeah, I see nothing beyond you," Karen said sarcastically. "Question, Buddy. Who are they?" Karen said in the same soft tone as Buddy's. Buddy suddenly got up in a jerk, pulled its tail out of Karen's hands and lashed it on her nose. Its body was in Karen's face and it said, "won't tell you, Karen. Nope, I won't. You got to tell me my scientific name first before I let you know more about my world."

"Ok, ok…got it. It's a deal. How about if I find out your scientific name for you and then come back and tell you. And then you can take me for a cruise of your world and tell me a little bit about it," Karen asked, looking straight at Buddy who had retracted its body away from Karen as she talked.

"Hmmmm…sounds like a good deal," Buddy said thoughtfully. "OK."

"That's good," Karen said happily and then continued, "Give me a five," and raised her hands. Buddy gave her a tail lash on her hands and they both laughed.

They passed by a lot of other shapes and also shapes that were identical to Buddy's except different in size. They kept swooshing and Karen saw some light. They were moving towards the light. Karen started to see hundreds of thousand of different shapes.

"These all your people?" Karen asked.

"Yep," Buddy replied and kept moving. A lot of them were gliding by individually, a lot of them were attached to each other like beads on a string, a lot of them were in a group crowded over big gooey-like shapes that were black in color.

"What is that?" Karen said pointing to the gooey-like shapes. She was hoping against all odds that Buddy would answer her, at least this time.

"Not fair, will tell you when you tell me my scientific name," Buddy said.

"As I expected," Karen muttered to herself. There were a lot of other shapes on big gooey pieces that looked like they were stuck against the side of the flask.

Buddy stopped moving and then said, "OK….I was thinking how are you going to find out what my scientific name is?" Buddy asked. "What do you do to find out my scientific name?" Buddy continued.

"Well, I will look for you first on the petri plate and then I will plate you to get a pure culture of you," said Karen, when Buddy interrupted her.

"How would you look for me?" Buddy asked.

"Your color and shape on the plate and it might or might not be different from other microbes or you might simply not be there on the plate which means you are present in a very low population density or you might not be cultivatable," Karen said.

"That doesn't always help then," Buddy said.

"Nope," Karen replied.

"Continue on," Buddy said.

"Then using the pure culture, if I have any, I will extract the DNA and then profile the DNA using a software to find out who you possibly are and how related you are to other bacteria. If I don't have the pure culture or can't find you on the plate, then I will extract DNA from the flask where we are. But that won't really pinpoint you. I mean you might be there like so many pins in a haystack but I won't really know which pin you are," Karen replied.

"Well, what if we are a new species, will the software detect us?" Buddy asked.

"Nope, it will say unknown but will give us how related your DNA profile is to other microorganisms," Karen answered.

"That's no guarantee that your method will help find my scientific name," Buddy said. "First, what if you don't find me on the plate? What if I just don't grow on your plates? Second, what if I am not common but something new and the software cannot detect me?" Buddy said, sounding desperate.

"Well, that's right. But that's the method we commonly use to identify microbes," Karen said.

"But not all microbes grow on plates, right?" Buddy asked.

"No," replied Karen.

"How many microbes have you scientists in the whole world identified?" Buddy asked.

"Less than 1%," Karen replied.

"Holy cow! That's it and you kill your ass off using that method? Can't you devise a better way to identify more microbes?" Buddy asked.

"Well, the DNA extraction method works because we don't have to grow you but on the other hand, the DNA method might not always ID you. Like I said, you might be one of the many needles in the haystack," Karen explained.

"But you said that you will find my scientific name," Buddy exclaimed.

" I will try," Karen replied.

"Oh yeah….find me on a stupid plate. You might not be able to recognize me from the others or I simply won't grow on the plate. And then that software will probably not be able to tell you who I am. That's your method," Buddy retorted madly, while gliding furiously in front of Karen. "That's no guarantee that you will find my scientific name," Buddy said and lashed its tail on Karen's nose.

"That's true. Research is not perfect like anything else in life, Buddy. We can only try and then move on from there," Karen replied. There were a lot of rod-shaped, tanned bacteria like Buddy all around them. But wait a minute. There were a few that had no flagella. "Hey Buddy, is something wrong with these guys? They broke their legs? Or are they not one of you and another kind of bacteria?" Karen asked, curiously.

"Won't tell you right now," Buddy exclaimed. "First you tell me my scientific name and then we will continue on from there," Buddy said.

Oh well, Buddy is not going to tell me anything about this fascinating world, Karen thought to herself. *If only I can find Buddy's scientific name, imagine how much I can learn about this world. I am in my culture flask with a talking microbe and imagine how much I can learn about my research this way,* Karen kept thinking when Buddy snapped her out by gently rubbing its flagellum on her nose.

"Ok, I have an idea. Here, you take all these guys," Buddy said, as he hurled some of the rod-shaped, tanned look-alikes at her. They bumped on her head like beach balls.

"Ewww," Karen said. They were stinky. They smelled very soily, more than ever.

"Well, you can extract their DNA to find my scientific name. You can also keep a little of them and try to grow them. Just hold onto their tails with your hands," Buddy said. That sounded like a good idea.

"Ok, that might work," Karen said. "Now get me out of here," she continued.

"Rub against the flask, downward three times with your right palm," Buddy said.

"I can't! Can't you see I am holding your kinds in both my hands?" Karen said.

"Well hold with one hand only," Buddy replied.

Karen let go of her left hand. She looked at her right hand. She was just holding two of them. "That's probably not enough for my work," she said. "Hey, you three. Come here," she looked at the three Buddy look-alikes in front of her. One of them came near her and said in a scared voice, "where will you take us?"

"You all are part of a BIG sample for Karen's research," Buddy retorted. "Now get close to her so she can grab your tails, will you?"

"I think we will be killed!" said a voice. Karen heard it from one of the look-alike whose tail she was holding.

"Maybe," Buddy replied. Suddenly, the tails Karen as holding onto slipped from her hands and the look-alikes ran away from her.

"Now what?" Karen asked Buddy, sounding mad."OK, how about if I dump them here and a lot more?" Buddy grabbed the rod-shaped, tanned bacteria from her hands and tried to squeeze them in her lab coat's pocket. They hardily fit in.

And then it plucked some more of these creature as most of them were more or less the same size as Karen.

"This is stinky," Karen replied.

"You are trying to kill us, Buddy," said a voice from one of the look-alike whose tail Buddy was trying to squish in Karen's lab pocket. It tried to wiggle out and then it was loose and quickly moved away.

"Babies, babies….wohooo! wohooo! come to Daddy. Come on, sweetie," Buddy said.

Suddenly, there were tiny Buddy look-alikes. Very small. They were all around Buddy.

"Get in there, you sweet babies," Buddy said, pointing with its flagellum to the pocket of Karen's lab coat. They snuggled in.

"I guess that will work," Karen said.

Suddenly, Buddy was very close to Karen's face and whispered in a firm tone, "Don't dare to talk about being alive or dead. Just know that I can make more babies. But don't scare them now."

Then Buddy's flagellum moved towards Karen's nose and before it could rub her nose, Karen replied, "Alright, got it…alright, now don't dare to rub it on my nose again.

Please!" Buddy moved away.

Karen looked through the shiny wall from where the light was coming. She saw huge things moving and looked at them carefully.

It was Marcus. *What a giant!* Karen thought. He wasn't that big but that was because she was so small she was in the flask, more or less the same size as Buddy. Would she be normal size when she got out of the flask? Would she get out of the flask in the first place? She thought. *I better get out when Marcus is not looking.* She kept looking at him and then saw him walk out of the door. Buddy kept looking at Karen and then Marcus.

"Gone, huh?" Buddy said.

"Yeah, I don't want anyone to know what is going on here," Karen said. "Hey Buddy, can you give me a quick tour of around the flask to see if anyone else might be in the lab?" Karen asked.

"You stupid? My babies are in your pocket. My babies. If I move around with you, they will fall out of the pocket and I am not chasing them," Buddy said. Buddy was right. Karen had on a typical lab coat with open pockets. "Don't you have lab coats with zippered pockets?" Buddy asked.

"I don't think so," Karen replied. "But I can have my Mom make zippered pockets on my lab coat for the next time I come over," Karen said.

"Just stay here and I will make sure there is no one around," Buddy said. Buddy zoomed off. It was gone in a blink and reappeared in a blink too! "Done. No one around in the lab," Buddy said.

"How did you manage to look around the flask so fast?" Karen asked, surprised at Buddy.

" I am a bacterium. Not a slow moving organism like you. Buddy replied proudly. "I gave you a ride in this flask as slowly as I could, my dear friend," Buddy said.

"I see," Karen said.

"Alright, you better get back to your lab before someone comes in," Buddy said and lashed its tail against her face. "That's a goodbye kiss," Buddy said, laughing. Karen grinned at Buddy and said, "Thanks, Buddy. I will see you again," and started rubbing her right palm downward on the flask, three times.

Suddenly, Karen felt herself being pulled out. She went swooooosh and it felt just like when she came in. Except instead of being pulled into a vacuum cleaner, she was being pushed out. Swooooosh. The darkness left her and there was bright light in front of her. And she was being pushed. The light got brighter and she was twirling and kept feeling the push. The air felt cooler. She closed her eyes shut, as tight as she could. This never happened to her and it was all scary but exciting. But she was hoping for a safe entrance out of the flask without getting hurt. Swoooosh, she kept twirling, the light got brighter, and the air kept feeling cooler. There was nothing to grab on to. Karen had her eyes closed and her hands spread out.

The suddenly, it was all calm. No swooshing sound, no pushing feeling. It felt brighter and cooler. Karen's feet felt something solid under them. She felt disoriented. She opened her eyes. Bingo! She was in her lab, she was standing on solid floor next to her culture flask, the same flask she had disappeared into. And she was of normal size, not a miniature self. Karen took a deep breath. She felt so relieved. And so alive. What an experience!

Karen looked into her lab pockets. Ewww! There was a thick, tan-color smear in her pocket. A thick smear. Karen recalled that Buddy had smeared its babies on her lab coat's pocket. Karen recalled that when she was in the flask, it didn't look like a smear but little Buddy babies. They were rod shaped, tanned in color, with one flagellum each. Just like Buddy. And here it was nothing more than a smear in her pocket.

Karen was deep into her thoughts about the adventure in the flask as she grabbed a sterile 50mL Falcon tube and then a spatula. She poured some 0.01% physiological saline into the sterile Falcon tube and then turned on the Bunsen burner. She didn't want anyone to see what she was doing. Scooping bacteria into the Falcon tube from her pockets of thick smear? No one does that. She dipped the spatula into 70% ethanol, shook off the excess alcohol and then flamed the spatula on the tip of the blue flame of the Bunsen burner. A red, high flame came out. She made a flagging motion with the spatula in the air to cool or else it might melt the plastic Falcon tube. She did that for a few seconds and then, holding the spatula in one hand, she used the palm of that hand to grasp the screw cap of the tube and using the other hand, she turned the tube until the cap came off. She carefully laid the cap face side down on the bench and gently touched the spatula against the side of the inside rim of the Falcon tube to make sure that the spatula was not too hot. If it was too hot, then it could kill the bacterial cells in the smear. But she didn't really need to do that as she had a lot of thick smear. Looked like custard but stinky. She scooped up the smear with the spatula and collected it in the Falcon tube. She scooped up more, and then more. She heated her spatula over the Bunsen burner once again when it cooled down completely. She didn't want any cross contamination. After she was sure that the spatula was not too hot, she scooped up some more of the smear. She kept doing it until she got most of the smear from her pocket. She screwed the cap on the tube and turned off the Bunsen burner. Then she vortexed the tube to mix the physiological saline solution with it. It turned tanned-color. She opened the tube and added some more saline solution to the 50mL mark, closed the tube, vortexed it, and put it on a scale in a small beaker. She labeled the tube BL and then Karen. "BL" for "Buddy Longtail". She found an empty 50mL Falcon tube and filled it with a bit of distilled water and put it on the other end of the scale in another small identical beaker. She kept pouring water and then closing the lid until the scale balanced. This was an important step because she was then going to centrifuge the tube. And for centrifugation, there had to be two tubes 180 degrees from each other of the same mass to balance the centrifuge. If not, the centrifuge would not be balanced, would make a horrid noise, possibly stop, and the material in the tube would not spin at an even angle and possibly also damage the centrifuge or the samples. She found the rotor that fit the Falcon tubes and screwed it the centrifuge. She put her two tubes at 180 degrees position from each other and put the rotor lid on. She closed the lid of the centrifuge and pressed 15,000 for rpm for 15 minutes. The centrifuge started, making a slight sound like that of the grass mower. The sound then gradually died and it was a gentle swoosh. The sound was just like when Karen was being swooshed into and out of the flask.

Karen looked at her lab coat. It was stinky. She better change her lab coat before anyone noticed the stink and the smear on the pockets. She hurried out of the lab into her office. It was dusk outside as she passed through the wall window. How long had she been in the flask? She didn't remember. Well, next time she better note the time she went on and came out. There had to be a next time. This was all so exciting. Karen was deep in this thought with her head down and didn't see Marcus coming towards her.

"Hey, Karen," Marcus said and Karen got startled out of her thoughts.

"Phew! You scared me," Karen said with her hands on her chest.

"As always," Marcus laughed. This was typical. Karen was a deep thinker and could go so deeply into her thoughts that she was oblivious of the existence of the world around her until people startled her out of her thoughts.

"Hey, there is fresh Taq today," Marcus said.

"Great," Karen said. "I better run to the rest room," she trailed off and then stopped to take off her lab coat. She dumped it in the dirty lab coats laundry basket that was in the corner of the hallway, near the recycle paper bin. She washed her hands, ran to her office space to put on a fresh lab coat, and then hurried off the lab. She had to finish washing off the centrifuged sample. For this, she poured off the liquid from the Falcon tube, added fresh physiological saline to 50mL mark, vortexed the tube, and centrifuged. She did this two more times. Then she scooped the pellet into two eppendorf tubes using a sterile inoculating needle. She would use this for culturing. She stored both tubes with the pellet in the freezer with her initials and date on them. Marcus was in the lab all the while to clean the glassware. They laughed and also did their own work. He left soon, just as Karen was done with the washing for the smear.

As Karen picked up the culture flask to move it to the corner, she thought about Buddy Longtail. She peered into the flask and said, "Hi, Buddy and lookalikes. I am back safe into the lab and I will come back after I find out your scientific name." She glanced at the flask for a while, looking for some reaction. Nothing. "Never mind, I will try to go in the flask again," Karen said, and moved the flask into the corner.

As Karen was walking home later on, she thought about the excitement of the day and couldn't wait to extract the DNA, find Buddy's scientific name, and go back into the flask for some adventures with Buddy. She went to the gym with Andy and then had dinner. She was all excited about her adventure in the flask and when she told Andy, he laughed it off calling it one of her imaginations.

"But imagine how cool your research would be if that was possible," Andy said.

Karen smiled. "It really happened, Andy. I am not kidding. I have a thick smear from Buddy Longtail's babies from my lab coat stored into two tubes in the lab and I can show you," Karen asserted.

Andy was laughing hard and said, "you sure that the smear didn't come from you? A boogie from your nose, maybe?" Andy knew Karen's obsession with her research work. The room was filled with peals of laughter from both of them.

Chapter 3

The World Of The Micro-Buddies

Karen sat back into her office chair and stretched out her arms. She glanced into her Cnergy coffee. It was still about two-thirds full. Cold coffee. No, she didn't want any more coffee. She already had a cup of coffee for the afternoon. Karen wasn't a heavy coffee drinker. A half cup in a morning, the afternoon and in the early evening was good enough for her. Medium-roast coffee with 2% milk in it and no sugar. Any more than that made her nauseous.

Amy had stopped by her office earlier that afternoon. She was on her way to get some coffee and Karen joined her for a breather. She had been at her desk all morning. She had been awake late last night. She had been at her desk all the time the day before. At the desk at home. At the desk at work. Except for a little chit-chat, gym, eating and sleeping, she had been at her desk, hard at analyzing the results that she got for Buddy's identification.

She had been working with the smear ever since she got back two weeks ago from the adventure in the flask. She plated the smear she got from the flask after washing it with physiological saline solution. She tried nutrient agar.

Karen tried full strength nutrient agar to grow the smear. She heated the inoculated loop, waited for a few seconds for it to cool off before picking up a little bit of the smear on it and swabbing the surface of the petri plate. She closed the plate and put it lid-side down on the bench at room temperature for 24 hours. Nothing grew. She tried the same thing but this time used a different incubation temperature of 37 degrees Celsius. She thought about using other high or low incubation temperatures. *But the flasks were incubated at room temperature and Buddy Longtail and its colonies were alive there*, Karen thought. So room temperature incubation was most realistic for growth, but only because Karen had her adventure in the flask and met Buddy Longtail. Without that, she would have been like any other scientist, trying out different incubation temperatures and different growth media.

But Karen did try diluted nutrient agar medium of 1:10 and 1:100 dilutions. No growth. So, Buddy Longtail and its colonies wouldn't grow on nutrient agar medium. Then one day, while looking at the flask with Buddy Longtail in it, it occurred to Karen, *"this is mineral salt medium. Why am I trying nutrient medium?"* Nutrient medium is a very common medium for the cultivation of non-fastidious organisms and so, when Karen had to grow colonies of Buddy Longtail to be able to identify it, nutrient medium automatically came in her mind. So she made mineral medium with crude oil as the carbon source, the same ingredients as in the flask, except she also used agar to provide a solid surface for growth.

No growth occurred on full strength mineral salt medium despite waiting for two weeks. So Karen tried dilutions. She started with 1/10 strength. Bingo! Twenty four hours later, the plates kept on the bench had colonies of Buddy Longtail. Tan with smooth edges.

"Hey, Buddy Longtail babies… hello!" Karen was so thrilled to see the growth. She kept the colonies pure and growing by sub-culturing onto fresh mineral agar plates with crude oil as the carbon source. This she did by picking up a colony, isolated from other colonies on the plate, with a sterile inoculating loop and swabbing it on a fresh mineral salt agar plate.

Karen used the pure colonies for morphological characterization and biochemical tests. She observed that the edges of the colonies were smooth. The colonies were tan colored. She also used these colonies to see if they would stain purple or pink using a test called the Gram stain. Karen had to take care not to spill the reagents on her as they stained purplish and red and stayed for a while, no matter how much soap or alcohol was used to scrub them off from the hands and clothes. Buddy Longtail colonies were negative for gram staining, as seen under a light microscope. The cells were rod shaped and each had a flagellum coming out from one end. But this alone would not help in identification for genus and species levels, as many bacteria can stain pink and have a rod shape with a flagellum. Further tests were needed.

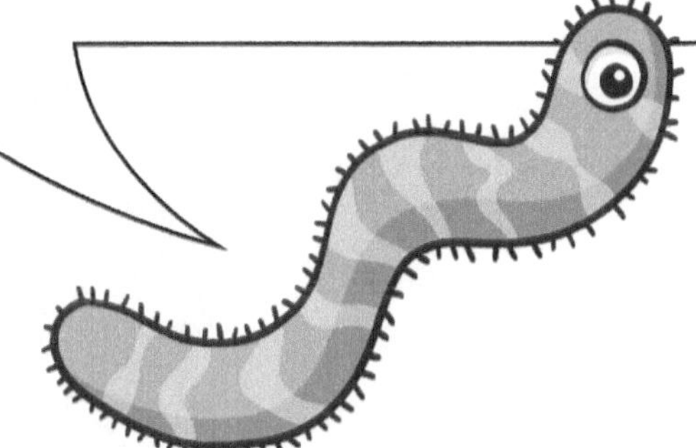

The results from the gram staining can be used in kits that give qualitative results for bacterial identification. Karen suspected that Buddy Longtail was a Pseudomonad because of the earthy smell from it and also from the colonies on the petri plates grown from the smear. However, despite doing the test several times, the identification chart could not identify Buddy Longtail colonies. The results simply didn't match up to any of the listed bacteria in the identification chart.

Qualitative test kits for bacterial identification

These kits contain strips. The strips consist of tiny clear microtubes containing dehydrated food. Bacteria, grown in a liquid medium, are added in these microtubules. The growth medium that comes along with the bacteria in the microtubules hydrates the food. The strips are incubated and if the bacteria metabolize the food in the microtubules, color changes occur. These color changes are recorded and are used for an identification chart or software to give the possible genus and species for the bacteria. The most common was the API20E strip kit for the identification of Enterobacteria and other gram negative rods including some Pseudomonads.

Karen then tried the molecular approach to identify Buddy Longtail colonies. She extracted the genomic DNA using a commercial kit. Then she loaded and ran the DNA extract on electrophoresis using agarose gel.

Agarose gel electrophoresis

DNA has a net negative charge due to the sugar-phosphate backbone and when electric current is passed in the process of electrophoresis, it migrates to the positive end of the electric field. The DNA, which is a colorless molecule, can be visualized by adding a dye to the gel or to the DNA sample. A commercial DNA marker is also loaded in the agarose gel. This marker has DNA fragments of known size, typically ranging from 125 base pairs to 23 kilo base pairs and can be used as a reference to find the size of the extracted DNA. DNA is a long, linear double helix but when extracted, it can break into fragments.

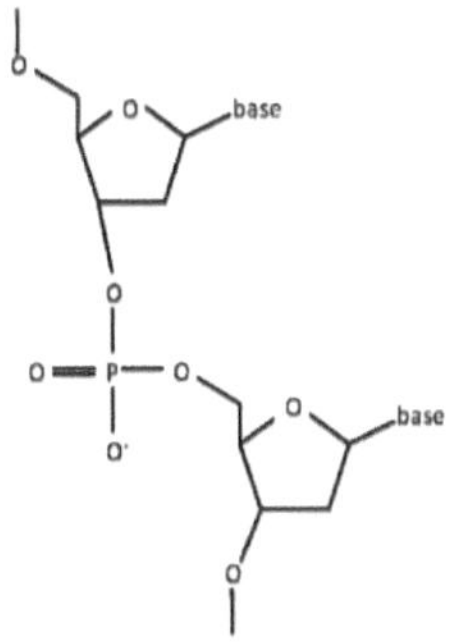

This she did to ascertain that the DNA was extracted and to have a visual picture of how much was extracted. Karen saw a faint band of about 2 kilo base pairs, which was what she expected. She also did a DNA concentration and purity tests by using the spectrophotometer to get the absorbance values at wavelength of 260 and 280. Then she used formulae for calculations to get the concentration and purity of DNA. She had approximately 200ng/μL of DNA which was good and the DNA sample was pure. Next, she did the polymerase chain reaction (PCR) with the extracted DNA sample using the thermocycler. Karen ran the PCR products for the 16S amplification on the agarose gel and visualized it using ethidium bromide staining and a DNA ladder that consisted of fragments of known size to recognize the size of the DNA fragments. She saw a band of 1.5kb in size, which is what she expected. The positive control also came out good, about this size.

Polymerase chain reaction (PCR)w

This is a commonly used technique in molecular biology to make millions of copies of a particular DNA sequence, in this case the 16S ribosomal DNA (rDNA) sequence. This region of the DNA was commonly copied because it contains conserved regions that allow primers to bind to help in amplification. It also contains hypervariable regions that can provide signature identification of bacterial species.

Next, she proceeded to do cloning using the PCR product. Karen incubated her plates for 18 hours at 37°C, the recommended incubation time. She had lots of white isolated colonies and a few blue colonies. The control, that had water in place of the PCR product, had lots of all blue colonies.

That was good and what she expected.

Agarose gel electrophoresis

While PCR does amplify the gene region into millions of copies, more copies of it are needed to eventually identify the letter codings of the DNA sequence. This is done by cloning.

For cloning, Escherichia coli (E.coli) cells are commonly used as the host cells along with a plasmid that could take in the PCR product. The PCR product is first purified to remove any contaminants or reagents from PCR left behind during the process. A plasmid is a circular piece of DNA and has genes on it that can confer special properties such as antibiotic resistance and bioluminescence properties to the organism. It can also be cut open, the PCR linear product can stick on it and the plasmid can close back with the help of enzymes. Calcium chloride and heat shock (putting the tubes with the material) is used to weaken the membrane so that the plasmid can enter through it. The cells with the plasmid, called competent cells, are then plated on agar plates. Not all cells will take up the plasmids and not all plasmids will take up the PCR products. The colonies on the agar plates are screened qualitatively. The agar plates contain ampicillin, an antibiotic. The plasmid used in transformation contains the genes for ampicillin resistance. Kanamycin can also be used in place of ampicillin. E.coli does not have ampicillin resistance and will not grow on agar plates with ampicillin. But if it has taken in the plasmid, the plasmid will confer ampicillin resistance to E.coli and it will be able to grow on the agar plates containing ampicillin. The insertion of the PCR product in the plasmid disrupts the gene expression for β-galactosidase and this leads to white colonies on the plate. Without the PCR product, the plasmid produces β-galactosidase which hydrolyzes 5-bromo-4-chloro-3-indoyl- β-D-galactoside, a dye, on the plate. The hydrolysis changes the dye to a blue color and so the colonies appear blue on the plate.

Performing cloning on PCR products prior to sequencing is done in some labs while other labs only perform the cloning step if the PCR product appears faint on the agarose gel, which means low PCR product yield. Some studies show that the entire PCR product is sequenced when using the plasmid, but some losses occur when the PCR product is directly sequenced. Other studies show no effects on the sequencing quality, whether directly from PCR to sequencing or having cloning as an intermediate process.

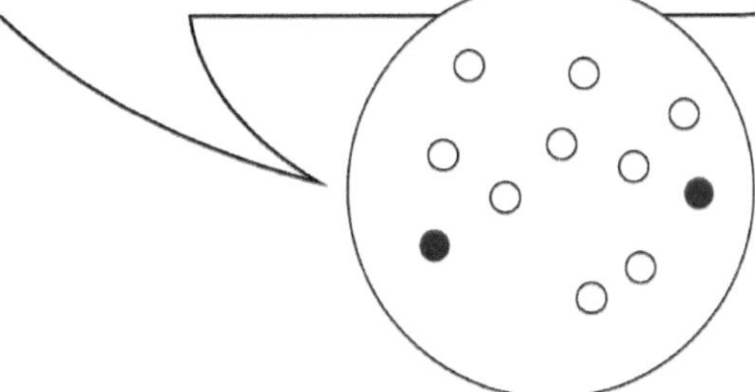

Isolation of recombinant plasmid DNA from
cloning and its preparation for sequencing

This is done by lysing the collected cells from centrifugation with sodium hydroxide and sodium dodecyl sulfate, a common detergent. These lyse the cell to let the plasmid out. The sodium hydroxide also serves to denature the chromosomal and plasmid DNA. Then is the neutralization step to allow the plasmid DNA to re-anneal and get back to its circular form. However, the complementary strands of the linear chromosomal DNA will not re-anneal properly and will be irreversibly denatured and insoluble. The neutralization solution contains potassium ions that cause the detergent to precipitate with the denatured, insoluble cell material including the chromosomal DNA. This precipitate is removed by centrifugation, leaving behind the plasmid DNA which is then used for sequencing.

Dr. Rogers' lab used the ABI sequencer for sequencing. Sometime there are gaps in the sequencing results which are represented by an N and in this case, the sequence needs to be edited to cut out the gaps. In case there are too many gaps, then the sequencing or the steps leading up to the sequencing are revised. Karen looked at her sequence-looked good!

ABI sequencing

This employed dye-terminator sequencing, automated protocol and the use of capillary electrophoresis. The techniques work like PCR and use a fluorescently labeled nucleotide that, when it binds to the template DNA for sequencing, fluoresces and makes the elongation process of DNA stop. Then the mixture of strands, all of different length and ending with a fluorescently labeled nucleotide, are separated by capillary electrophoresis, the results of which can be visualized on an attached computer in the form of peaks for the fluorescence. Each of the four nucleotides is labeled with a different colored fluorescence, allowing the sequence to be read on the computer.

The next step was to copy and paste the sequence into a sequencing database. There are several of them available, some free on the web. The sequence is then compared to other sequences in the database to identify the organism. Karen did this search and waited…and waited. Sometimes, it can take a few minutes. Then came the results. Unknown organism. She looked at the percent similarity to other organisms. The closest it came to was to *Pseudomonas stutzeri*, but….only about 35% related. Oh well, Buddy Longtail. Rod shaped, tanned, a single flagellum. It smelled soily, a characteristic odor of Pseudomonad. But Karen's guess was wrong. Growth and biochemicals tests were different for *Pseudomonas stutzeri* and Buddy Longtail and molecular identification indicated that the two were different species. What could it be?

Karen liked the name, Buddy Longtail. Karen missed Buddy and its spunky nature. She particularly missed riding in the flask by holding on to its tail. It had been a month since she visited the flask and she wanted to go in again. It was Friday, a quiet day when people also left early for the weekend. This was a good time for Karen to meet Buddy again. Oh, how she missed being the flask. She missed Buddy. But, she didn't have any good news for Buddy. She didn't know Buddy's scientific name.

Karen kept rubbing the culture flask. She couldn't go in as she did the first time. Circular rubs. Nothing happened. Her palms were sweaty. She had been trying for an hour. What was the magic rub? She stroked the flask with slow downward motion with her right palm. One time. Two times. Three times. And she got whisked in. So that was the magic rub. Rub in downward stroke three times with your right palm. It was the same sensation she had before. The whisking in feel as if being sucked by a vacuum cleaner. All dark. Soily smell. In and in she went. This time she was all familiar with the feeling. Dark, weightless, floating around… then suddenly there was a big whoosh on her face.

"Might be Buddy's flagellum," Karen thought. Whoosh, it went. Then again and again, and it kept going on as if a rope was gently lashing against her from different directions. As her eyes got adjusted to the darkness, she saw the tan, rodshaped figure moving around her and going whoosh.

"Hey, Buddy," Karen said excitedly. Whoosh, it went on her face. "How are you doing?" she asked. No answer. Whoosh. And whoosh and so on. "Hey Buddy, I'm soooo happy to see you." Whoosh it went on her face. "Hey," and whoosh it went again. It just kept whooshing her even when she was silent. No support under her feet or on her hands. She felt drifting. And the whooshing kept going on. Whoosh… whoosh, on her face. And she could feel the slime on her face. She used her hands to wipe off the slime and whoosh it came back on her.

"Come on, Buddy…that's enough," said an irritated Karen.

Whoosh. "BUDDY, ENOUGH!" yelled Karen. Whoosh.

Then she heard someone laughing.

"Hee, hee, hee, hee…wooooow, hoo, hoo, hoo, hoo, hee, hee," and then a whoosh again.

"Stop," yelled Karen. She was irritated by now. "Hee, hee, hee, hee, wooow, hee, hee, hee". It sounded like a whole group of something laughing. Then there was silence. Suddenly, she saw a rod-shaped, tan figure right in front of her face. It moved past her face very swiftly.

"Poor Karen," a voice said. It was Buddy! She recognized the manly voice. But there were two of them. One bigger, one smaller. Which one was Buddy? One of them? Or maybe Buddy wasn't there and they were some other creatures. "So, which one am I?" the voice said. "Point!" it continued. Karen was puzzled. She would need to guess. She pointed to the big creature. The voice was audible and all that big, slimy lashing couldn't have been from the small creature. "I knew you would pick Tupac," the voice said as the smaller creature moved to Karen. Whoosh, it went with its flagellum. And then it stopped with the flagellum in front of it.

"Here. I am Buddy. Hold this flagellum," the rod-shaped, tanned creature in front of Karen said.

"So the other one is Tupac?" Karen asked as she glided through the flask, holding onto the flagellum.

"Yep," replied Buddy.

"So, how do I know you apart from the other identical creatures?" Karen asked.

"No, we are not all identical," Buddy said and then stopped moving. "Look at my border and compare that with Tupac," Buddy said. Karen looked at it closely. Buddy's border also had turf-like structures and so did Tupac's border. She looked more closely. Buddy's border had obviously more places with two "short strands" coming out together at the same locations but Tupac's border had less of these. Karen thought about the membrane structure. It was a fluid-mosaic structure of phospholipids. And coming out of it were biochemicals including glycoproteins. Glycoproteins were carbohydrates attached to proteins! So those "short strands" were carbohydrates and they were attached by covalent bonds to proteins that were embedded in the membrane.

Karen thought about people and how all human beings have the same physical attributes: eyes, nose, mouth, ears, legs, arms. But two people are different from each other based on the little differences in the attributes. Take the eyes for example. Big eyes, small eyes, round eyes, squinty eyes.

Same for the other physical attributes. Of course, you have pigment variations. Blonde hair, blue eyes and so on. Two people can have blonde hair and blue eyes but they don't look identical because the physical attributes have different sizes and shapes and also slightly different locations. These differences are what distinguish two people from each, other although all human belong to the species *sapiens*. So it was the same in Buddy's world. Members of Buddy's species were not identical like what Karen observed. The carbohydrate locations and their numbers on the proteins in the membranes could set two members apart from each other. Buddy's membrane had two carbohydrate chains clumped together at one of the membrane proteins while Tupac's membrane had less of these.

Karen thought about taxonomic classification for Buddy and Tupac. Sure, they would have identical taxonomic classification, making them one species. It was like taxonomic classification for two human beings. Let's say both have blue eyes and blonde hair. DNA profiling from their blood sample will place them at the species, sapiens. But they will look different because of the differences in the physical attributes. Same here with Buddy and Tupac. DNA profiling would place both Buddy and Tupac in the same species.

Karen thought about the carbohydrates contents for profiling microorganisms. Different microorganisms should contain different amounts of carbohydrates; it is one factor that could distinguish one species from another. Buddy and Tupac had differences in the arrangement of the carbohydrate on the membrane protein but the total amount of membrane carbohydrate would be the same, or relatively the same, for both of them. On the other hand, some species have a range concentration for chemical concentrations. So it could be that Buddy and Tupac had different concentrations of membrane carbohydrate but they fell in the range for their species. But overall, it was not only the carbohydrate content that distinguished Buddy's species from others. A lot of other chemical compositions are considered when doing the biochemical identification tests that Karen did earlier in an attempt to find out Buddy's genus and species name.

Karen looked at Buddy and Tupac closely. They were swirling around her and Karen tried to get hold of Buddy's flagellum but it slipped off her hands since Buddy was moving around.

"Hey Buddy, stop for a while, will you?" Karen said. Buddy stopped and said, "why? You want to go back to your world?!"

"No, I want to count the turfs and the blobs on you," Karen said.

"You what?" Buddy said and fell into a peal of laughter. "Count them? You heard that Tupac? This living thing wants to count our turfs and hills." Karen heard peals of laughter. They were both laughing, Buddy and Tupac. "Whoa, hee hee hee hee," they went.

"How are you going to do it, Karen?" Tupac asked. "You bought a device?" Buddy asked.

"No, I will use my eyes," Karen replied. And again, she heard peals of laughter. "What's so funny?" Karen asked.

"Nothing," Buddy said calmly and then the peals of laughter resumed. "Whooooaa, heee, heee, hee," it continued. This enraged Karen and made her more determined.

"Fine, keep laughing. Laugh it out with all your heart," she snapped.

"Heart? Heart? Whooooooooaa, hee, hee, hee. We have a heart?" Buddy said, laughing along with Tupac. The words just slipped out of Karen's tongue. It was her way of talking, what can she do? Then came a big, gentle lashing of the slimy flagellum. Ugghh!

Karen called out for Buddy and Tupac. She was floating. Nothing to hold onto! What a pain! "I need you both here," she wailed. Then she said, "Buddy, help! Give me your flagellum.". It appeared right in front of her. She grasped it.

"You are so confusing, Karen! First you want us in front of you to count our turfs and bumps. Then you want to hold onto my flagellum. What kind of a confusing creature are you?" Buddy commented tartly.

"I am sorry, Buddy. Tupac, I am sorry" Karen said, trying

to calm down. She took a deep breath. "OK, now I want you both in front where I can see you," Karen said.

"So that you can count our-" Buddy was cut short with a Shhhhhh sound from Karen.

"OK, in front," Karen ordered.

They swam and came to a standstill in front of her, Buddy's flagellum making a U-shape with Karen holding the end of it. Karen looked at Buddy's membrane carefully. There were so many of the glycoproteins. She couldn't count them. She rubbed her eyes with her free hand, the other one grasping Buddy's flagellum. She closed her eyes for a few seconds and then looked at the glycoproteins more carefully.

She tried counting them. She put her finger in front of her to block from her view the glycoprotein she started counting from. She was on number 57 and had spent at least five minutes when she lost track. Wow! There were so many. Her head was twirling from all the counting attempts. How many were there? Probably more than she could count.

"So, how is the counting going? ha ha.. Karen?," Buddy tried asking while giggling.

"Is this creature still counting?" came a squeaky voice. It was Tupac. "Why is it counting our turfs and bumps? Has it not gone mad yet?"

"This creature is a female human being, Tupac. Scientifically called *Homo sapiens*," Buddy replied, sounding pleased at its description of Karen.

"Watch this," Buddy continued.

While Karen was still holding onto Buddy's flagellum and was lost in her thoughts, Buddy wiggled its flagellum so that Karen's hands gently rubbed on it. Then swiftly, it put the tip of the flagellum in Karen's nostrils.

"Ha ha ha," Tupac squealed. Then Tupac did the same, it put its flagellum on Karen's nostril.

"STOP IT," Karen roared. Then she let go of Buddy's flagellum and rubbed her nose as hard as she could.

Buddy and Tupac got away from her. They were in a distance. It was dead quiet. Karen then realized her behavior. She missed being the flask, she missed Buddy. And she was so happy to meet Buddy. She realized that she was spending her time in the flask counting glycoproteins on Buddy and Tupac. *That's a stupid idea*, she thought. And it wasn't right of her to yell at Buddy and Tupac when all they wanted was to spend time with her and have some fun. She wanted the same. "I am sorry," Karen said.

"That's ok, Karen. My sweet friend, Karen," Buddy said softly.

"Yeah," replied Tupac.

"Is that Tupac?" Karen asked.

"Yeah, that is Tupac. Sounds cute, eh?" Tupac's voice was squeaky compared to Buddy's, who had a manly voice.

"Yeah," said Karen.

"Now hold my flagellum and we will go for a ride. What do you say?" Buddy asked. Karen nodded and quietly put her hands on the flagellum.

"So, did you find out my scientific name?" Buddy asked excitedly.

"Well- " Karen was cut off by Buddy.

"Yes or no!? Or are you more idiotic than I thought?" Buddy asked.

"No," said Karen softly.

"Nnnn, no?" asked Buddy. "Why not? What were you doing for so long while I was wondering where you were? And what did you do with my babies that I gave you? Ate them!?" asked Buddy, sounding real mad.

"I used the smear and I tried every possible method out there to find out who you are. You are not related to *Pseudomonas stutzeri,*" explained Karen.

"Not related to *Pseudomonas stutzeri*?" asked Buddy.

"No," said Karen.

"You sure you tried every technique you know out there to find out my scientific name?" asked Buddy.

"Yes, I did," replied Karen.

"Then what am I?" Buddy retorted.

"Smear. Hee hee hee hee," laughed Tupac. "We are just a smear," said Tupac.

"No, Tupac. We are not a smear. We are intelligent creatures. Human beings can't live without us. Even Karen cannot live without us. This wimp cannot move around the flask without us," Buddy declared proudly.

"Yeah, me intelligent," said Tupac and gently lashed its flagellum at Buddy. Karen found Tupac cute.

"So, Karen, you are really, really sure that you tried out every possible method out there to find out my genus and species name?" Buddy asked.

"Yes, I am positive," replied Karen confidently.

Buddy stood frozen in front of Karen. It seemed like a very long time and finally when Karen got irritated, she said,

"Buddy, you ok?" No reply. "Buddy?"

"Yeah, I am here," came Buddy's reply.

"What's going on?" said Karen.

"Nothing, just making sure that you tried everything you know, everything possible to find out my scientific name and yet didn't come up with it."

"Buddy, I tried- "

Buddy lashed the flagellum at Karen and then said, "I know, I know".

Tupac sounded like it was crying. "We are going to die," it wailed.

"Die? Why? No one will die, Tupac, " said Buddy.

Tupac's shape squeezed into Buddy as if he was hugging him, "We don't know our name. We are going to DIE!! I don't want to die, Buddy, no," Tupac said.

Karen started giggling. She found it funny.

"Hey stop that, Karen," Buddy said, letting go of its flagellum from Karen's hands and then whipping its hard against her head.

At that point, Tupac's shape moved away from Buddy and Tupac said, "Bad, Karen, Buddy! Bad!" and started whipping Karen with its flagellum continuously.

"Eeeewwwwww," yelled Karen and started reaching out for Buddy's flagellum.

"Stop it, Tupac. Stop. She is not bad.," said Buddy and quickly went after Karen and offered her its flagellum so that she could hold onto it and not drift off. Karen quickly grabbed the flagellum and had second thoughts about Tupac.

Cute but can be naughty, she thought to herself.

"Now look Tupac, she doesn't knows our scientific name yet but she will find out later. Meanwhile, let's call us the Longtails. Buddy Longtail. Tupac Longtail," said Buddy.

"I agree," said Karen. They looked at Tupac.

"What do you say, Tupac? Tupac Longtail?" asked Buddy.

There was a pause and then Tupac said wearily, "OK, then Karen is Karen Notail." They all laughed.

"Alright then. So Karen will continue to find out our species name. Now since she is here and we don't know when she might be back, let's take her on a tour of our world. What do you say, Tupac?" asked Buddy.

"Ar we going to visit Rico?" asked Tupac.

"I guess we will see Rico anyway," answered Buddy.

"No Rico… no," whimpered Tupac. Rico was a mean bacterium who loved spewing on Tupac; Buddy and their species didn't like to be around it.

"Oh well… come on, she has to know," retorted Buddy.

"Who is Rico?" asked Karen curiously.

"This is Rico," Tupac jumped. It spat on Karen's face. A tiny spit on Karen. Felt like a drop of rain. Karen wiped it off with her left hand as she was using the right one to hold onto Buddy's flagellum. Then Tupac spat again. Then again. All on the face. Karen found that funny. Then, all of a sudden Tupac started flapping its flagellum as fast as it could, hitting it against Karen's butt. It was spanking her! And it continued spitting at the same time.

"That's Rico!!!! RICO!!!! That's what Rico does!!!! RICO!!! RICO!!!" yelled Tupac, flagellum whipping against Karen and little, teeny spit coming out at the same time. Karen was amazed. Hilarious. Tupac was so cute. She started laughing.

"OK, OK, enough," Buddy said, coolly. But Tupac continued lashing and spitting and Karen continued laughing. "ENOUGH!!" repeated Buddy. Karen stopped laughing but Tupac continued. Spitting and spanking. "TUPAC, heard me? ENOUGH," yelled Buddy. Suddenly, it was all quiet and still. "OK, so let's introduce our world to Karen. Should we, Tupac?" Buddy said.

"Yeah, lets goooo," Tupac said.

Karen glided through the darkness holding onto Buddy's flagellum. Buddy and Tupac were moving very slowly.

"Now pay attention, Karen," Buddy said.

"I see nothing, just darkness," replied Karen.

"Well, focus. Concentrate on what you see. Use your eyes," replied Buddy.

"Hee, hee, hee. Karen's got bad eyes. We got good eyes," said Tupac.

"You don't have eyes, silly," retorted Karen. "Bacteria don't have eyes," she continued. Buddy stopped and then turned to Karen.

"OK, Karen. Yes, we don't have what you guys call eyes. But we have sensors. Taxis sensors. To feel all that there is to feel. Including you! And that's how we navigate around," replied Buddy.

"Flagellum, chemical movement inside you, cell receptors," Karen added. Makes sense.

They glided through. Karen tried to focus on the darkness around her. Then Buddy stopped. Karen looked carefully at a big irregular shape with grooves coming out of it. It looked like something was moving in it. Looked like a Buddy- and Tupac-like creatures. Then there were other creatures of different shapes, some moving and some stuck.

"How are you doing there, Karen?" asked Buddy.

"OK," said Karen slowly.

"What do you think of our world so far?" Buddy asked. "Too dark," came Karen's reply.

As they glided through the darkness, Karen saw a little flick of light. It looked like a firefly. And then she saw more and more of them. Rod shaped with lots of flagella coming out at one place, called lopotrichous flagella arrangement in Biology. The rod shapes all had light in them, looking like fireflies on a clear, dark night. *Might be Vibrio fischeri or another bioluminescent bacteria*, Karen thought.

"Hey Bernie, how is it going?" Buddy asked, rubbing the tip of its single flagellum against the lopotrichous flagella on

Bernie

"Hey, Buddy!"

"Hey, Carrie," Buddy said.

"Howdy, Buddy," another voice said.

"Hey, Joey," Buddy replied.

"What's up?" a voice asked and whipped the turf of lopotrichous flagella all over Buddy like a mop. Buddy shook a little and then used its flagellum to wipe off.

"Hey Beanie, same old…same old Beanie," and they all started laughing. Then came, "heee heee hee," from Tupac. "Hey, Tupac," they all said and lashed their flagella all over Tupac. Tupac kept laughing while Karen held onto Buddy's tail. She could see them all clearly. Tupac was larger than Buddy. Both were rod-shaped and had a single long flagellum. Buddy's border had more of the "double turfs" (two glycoprotein strands coming out of one place) than Tupac's. Suddenly, Bernie and the other glowing bacteria were all around Karen, gliding a little and rubbing against her with their polar flagella. Beanie rubbed the turf of lopotrichous flagella like a mop on Karen.

"Hey come on Beanie, stop it," ordered Buddy.

"What is that?" Beanie said, circling Karen.

"It is an alien," replied Tupac in its squeaky voice. "An alien!" they all retorted.

"Come on, Tupac, you know better. This is Karen," replied Buddy.

"Karen. What is Karen?" asked Beanie.

"A human," replied Buddy and before Buddy could continue, Beanie said, "You bought a human alien into the flask!"

"OK, OK, calm down everyone! Karen is my friend, she is your friend too! She means no harm, she is a good human," explained Buddy.

"And how do you know that?" questioned Bernie. "Because I have seen her grow us, watched her from the flask and she is good," replied Buddy.

"Grow us? You are all dying, Buddy," retorted Bernie.

"Rico and Rico's fellows are starving you," continued Bernie.

"We are going to die," cried Tupac.

"Let me explain, let me explain," retorted Buddy. "And Tupac, shut up!! You heard me, shut up!! No one is going to die. BUT you are going to die if you keep saying it," yelled Buddy. Tupac started wailing and Carrie moved closer to Tupac and comforted Tupac with its lopotrichous flagella mop.

"You won't die, Tupac. We will all be OK," said Carrie soothingly.

"Yeah, we all live. Karen live too," said Tupac and in that instant, Tupac gently wiped its flagellum on Karen's face who was holding on steadily to Buddy's flagellum.

"Ok, so let's do the introduction. This is Karen. She is our human friend. Very smart," said Buddy.

"And funny too," quipped in Tupac and laughed.

"Yes, she is fun too," said Buddy. "Ok, now Tupac help me point out the fellows here, will you?" asked Buddy. "Ready," said Tupac. Tupac pointed out each one to Karen with its flagellum while Buddy spoke out the names. They all wiggled a little when introduced.

They were all different in size and appearance, just like people were different in little features that set them apart. They all had lopotrichous flagella and were bioluminescent. Bernie was the biggest, scruffiest looking and with the brightest luminescent. "Bernie is the lantern leader," explained Buddy. Carrie was about the same size as Bernie and bright as Bernie. But it had longer lopotrichous flagella compared to Bernie. Then in size was Joey, with dimmer brightness compared to Bernie and Carrie. Harry was the smallest one but with long lopotrichous flagella. Beanie was about Joey's size but brighter than Joey. It had small, thick lopotrichous flagella.

"Karen is our guest. We are going to show her our world. She is a microbial scientist. She grew us and came to visit us," explained Buddy.

"But your gang is dying," explained Beanie.

"I know, I know," cut in Buddy. "I know, my fellows, that we are dying. And showing Karen our world will help her help us," explained Buddy.

"How good of a scientist is she?" retorted back Bernie.

"I have watched her from the glassy surface of the flask. She works very hard. And she is friendly," explained Buddy.

"We are called the Longtails," quipped Tupac. "The Longtails?" asked Carrie.

"Sounds horrible," said Bernie and started mopping the polar flagella on Buddy.

"OK, Bernie, stop, STOP!" Buddy yelled. Bernie stopped. "Ok, Karen tried to find our name by all means using all that she knows what to do in her lab and she couldn't find our name. Which means we might be a new organism. Now isn't that exciting?" asked Buddy. There was dead silence. Then Bernie said, "I don't quite get it. How can it be exciting that we are a new organism?"

"Well, think. There is no one like us out there that scientists know. We will have a new name. We will be famous for being new," said Buddy. There were murmurs. "So Karen, do you share this excitement?" asked Bernie, shining its light in Karen's face.

Karen, still holding onto Buddy's flagella said, " I think so but I am not sure. I tried every method out there that we use to identify microorganisms and I can't find a match in the library that we have," explained Karen.

"She took some of my babies to do this research for finding our scientific name," added Buddy. By now, most microorganisms had swarmed around Karen and Buddy. Tupac stuck close to Buddy.

"Your babies? How can you trust her so easily, Buddy? How do you know that she didn't use them for her own selfish interest? or if the babies are not dead?" asked Bernie, circling Buddy.

" I have seen her work hard in the lab. Plus, if she does act selfish, you know that we can attack her," explained Buddy. Karen gulped. Attack her? Her mind started wandering into microbial infections. Imagine the flagella or secretion sticking on her skin and toxins being injected into her. Or they all grow in her skin, giving her lesions. She cringed at that thought. Wow, it was so hot in that flask!

"Makes sense," said Bernie. "And you will do exactly that, Buddy, or you lose us," continued Bernie.

"Of course, Bernie. You know that we all depend on you and your fellows. We can't live without you. All that decay will kill us and only you can take care of it," explained Buddy. The microorganisms all stopped swarming around Buddy and Karen.

"OK, Karen. You heard us. No betrayal or it is the end for you," warned Buddy. Karen swallowed hard. She could feel her palm slipping on Buddy's flagella. She was horrified and sweating.

"Yes, Buddy. I heard it. I don't want to die from an infection or any poison from you guys," said Karen weakly. "You won't, Karen," said Buddy immediately and soothingly.

"Just don't betray us or hurt us. Promise?" asked Buddy.

"I promise," replied Karen.

Tupac started dancing all around Karen. "Boogie, boogie, Longstails, boogie, boogie, Longtails," went Tupac. After saying boogie, it wiggled its body. After saying Longtails, its flagellum waved. Everyone was laughing hard, including Karen. She felt so much better.

"Here Karen, give me your hands, one at a time, I will wipe them," said Bernie. Karen gave Bernie her free hand and held it opened wide, palm side facing up. Bernie mopped the palm with its lopotrichous flagella. Karen's palm was all smeared. It smelled fishy.

"Ugh," came from Karen.

"Well, it will help you stick your hand on Buddy's flagellum," explained Bernie. "Now give me your other hand." Karen switched her hands, using the smeared one for holding Buddy's flagellum. It did give her a snug, firm hold on Buddy's flagellum.

As they all moved along with Karen holding Buddy's flagellum, Karen saw what looked like dark, irregular shaped rocks with grooves in them, stalagmite and stalactite-looking shapes jutting in and out of the grooves. Horizontal and also vertical from down. Karen and the micro-buddies were moving in between them in the open space in these "rocks". They were guided by the light from Bernie, Carrie, Joey, Harry and Beanie. Karen saw that there were a lot of creatures of different shapes, sizes and colors, most of them in the surface of the structures and a lot of them swarming in the grooves of the structures.

"What are these structures?" Karen asked Buddy.

"You don't know what these are?" retorted Buddy. "You are the one who dumped us and a dark liquid that turns into this structure when it is in the flask. "Now you tell me what this is," continued Buddy.

"It is yummy, yummy food!" replied Tupac.

"Shhhhh," replied Buddy. "I asked Karen, not you. Karen, look at it carefully," said Buddy. Karen looked at it closely. The "rocks" looked shiny and were blackish/brown and also reddish in some places. They had a mousse-like appearance. Karen tried to remember what she put in. Mineral salt medium and crude oil. Crude oil! So these blackish-brown "rocks" had to be crude oil.

"Oil?" said Karen.

"What do I know? It is just yummy food. Our food. Our fuel," replied Buddy.

Karen touched a bit of the "rock" in front of her. It felt mousy and it smelled just like oil. Then they went downward. They kept going downward in the groove tunnel, in the mousse. Then they went to the left. And there was a white light, which kept getting stronger as they kept moving left in the groove tunnel. Then they stopped.

"Look there," Buddy said, using its flagellum for a split second to point out and then giving it back to Karen to hold on to. Karen looked carefully. There was a huge, distorted image in front of her. As she tried figuring out what it was, Buddy said, "I see you sitting there for long hours." Then it occurred to Karen that it was her lab bench and she also saw her lab chair. So they were on the edge of the flask. The area was clear there. Karen looked around. They were in a mousse, near the edge of a groove and there was clear medium liquid around them. "So some organisms in the flask managed to eat this part of the mousse and that allowed us more spaces where we can stare at you," explained Buddy.

"You guys ate this?" asked Karen, surprised.

" It is a long story and I will tell you later on," Buddy replied with a deep breath. Karen looked at the clear glass of the flask. It felt cool and moist when she put her hand on it. She saw her hand print. Five fingers and a palm. But it started fading with the moistness. Must be very moist here, she thought. She felt her face and hairs with her hand. All wet. Eeewww! It smelled like soil and fish. She was surprised that she didn't feel the heat or the stinkiness all the while. Maybe because of the excitement. And also maybe because of the friendly, adorable microbes around her. She was truly enticed by all who she met and all that she saw in the flask. Karen looked carefully through the glass to see what was going on in the lab. There was Amy, moving a cart full of flasks. Everything looked so huge. Amy looked big, like a giant. She saw Amy put the flasks on the stirrer, adjust the setting there. Her fingers were huge, and she felt like a tiny ant in front of it.

Suddenly, Karen was jerked by Buddy.

"Move, fellows. FAST. FAST," yelled Buddy. Karen, holding tight onto Buddy's flagellum, was swirled in at lightning speed. She could see the skin on her hands forming ripple shapes because they were moving very fast. She saw Tupac, Bernie, Carrie, Joey, Harry and Beanie around her. Their flagella were lashing wildly.

"Watch out," yelled Buddy. A huge red rock was coming toward them. Buddy swerved under it, taking Karen along. Karen felt her body move down, and felt as if she was going to puke. The same feeling you get when the plane ducks down all of a sudden and very fast. Her heart was pounding. What could that be? All red? Insoluble iron? She remembered putting a bit of ferric chloride in the flask.

It was very bright. There were swarms of these Bernielike organisms and they seemed to grow in number as they kept moving.

"This sucks, Bernie. Do they all have to follow us? Rico and the gang can track us with the light movement," said Buddy, in a high-strung voice.

"You know how it is, Buddy. They collect in the light," answered Bernie. "And I can't beat them up, they are our people. That would be barbaric," continued Bernie. It was called quorom sensing, thought Karen. In quorom sensing, a stimulus leads to increased population density. In this case, the stimulus was light. Light from Bernie, Carrie, Joey, Harry and Beanie caused others like them to swarm together.

"Hey Buddy, how about if you all get into a hole and we will leave you alone," suggested Bernie. They were moving so fast and Karen was dizzy. It felt like skydiving except that rather than going straight down, the motion was irregular. Sometimes up, down, right, left, zigzag, down, down, up, zigzag and so on. Karen looked back and tried to focus. She couldn't see well. But she saw rod-shaped, yellow and tan colored organisms following them all. She couldn't see much more.

Suddenly, they were in a dark place and they stopped moving. Karen was nauseous and sweating. But still, she held onto Buddy's flagellum out of fear of being lost in nowhere.

"Here Karen, sit," Buddy said.

"I can't see," whimpered Karen.

"I know you can't see," said Buddy. "But sit here." Buddy moved its flagellum from her hand and Karen's hands felt a hard, cold surface. Karen sat down. Buddy was next to Karen and Tupac on her other side. Their flagella were resting on her lap. Cute sight! Karen focused on her breathing. She felt Buddy's flagellum wiping off the sweat from her forehead.

"What were we running from?" Karen asked in a wimpy voice.

"Monster! Wick monster! Bad Rico!" retorted back Tupac.

"That was Rico and Rico's gang?" asked Karen.

"Yep," replied Buddy. "They secrete this stuff that is a killer. And if it touches us, we start to die," explained Buddy. That's why they were running away.

"What about Bernie and Bernie's group? Do they die on contact with this chemical?" asked Karen.

"No, they don't. They are fine," replied Buddy.

"Where are they now?" asked Karen.

"Questions, questions and questions. I am tired, can't you see?" retorted Buddy.

"They are hiding, Karen, they are hiding," whispered Tupac. "They don't want to come in here or Rico will get us," explained Tupac, still in a whisper.

"Thank you, Tupac," said Karen and rubbed Tupac's flagellum. Karen felt the surface she was sitting on. Felt mousse-like. She smelled her hands. Ugh! Smelled like gasoline. They were inside an oil mousse. Buddy and Tupac were still, as if they were resting, and their flagella were still in Karen's lap.

Karen saw a flicker of light. It moved towards her and got brighter. Her heart started pounding. She felt for the flagella. They were gone. They were not in her lap. She looked around. Buddy was a little away from her with its flagellum wrapped around it, like a dog curled up for a sleep. Tupac was nowhere. Karen sat still, scared. She couldn't think. As the light came near her, the figure looked familiar. Rod shaped, lopotrichous flagella. It was Bernie!

"Bernie, I am so happy to see you," said Karen with relief. "You guys OK?" asked Bernie.

"Yeah, we are all OK," replied Buddy.

"And I thought you were sleeping," said Karen. "Bacteria sleep? Ha ha ha ha," laughed Buddy. "Now come on Karen, you are smarter than that. Bacteria sleep? We have a sleep cycle?" asked Buddy. Karen had never heard of a sleep cycle for bacteria. But they divided by binary fission.

"No," said Karen. "Where's Tupac?" she asked.

Bernie cast light on Tupac. Tupac was a few feet away from them and looked odd, kind of strange. Tupac's flagellum appeared hooked into the mousse. Karen observed carefully. A right-hand C shape formed in one place on Tupac cell wall and membrane. Outside of this shape, a dark liquid accumulated. The C-shape deepened and surrounded the dark material until it started to look like an almost closed O shape with the dark material inside it. Then the O shape was complete, the wall and membrane got back to normal shape. The O-shape was inside Tupac and the border of it was surrounded by cell wall and membrane. Inside of this border was the dark material. The O-shape and the dark material slowly faded away. This was pinocytosis, which means that Tupac was drinking the dark liquid.

Then Karen observed something else also occurring with Tupac. A pale yellowish liquid accumulated near the cell membrane in Tupac. It was surrounded by a cell wall and membrane which fused with the side of the cell, causing the cell's membrane and wall to bulge out. Then the pale yellow liquid was pinched off from the cell. This was exocytosis, excretion. So Tupac was eating and peeing at the same time. *Maybe Tupac is eating and drinking, pooping, and peeing, all at the same time,* Karen thought.

Beside pinocytosis and exocytosis, chemicals can move in and out of the cells by facilitated diffusion and active transport using protein carriers. Maybe I need to look more closely at Tupac to observe these mechanisms. That will be so awesome, Karen thought.

"Move it, Charlie," yelled Tupac. Karen snapped out of her thoughts. Tupac's flagellum came out of the hole in the mousse where it was anchored, whipped something next to it and then quickly went back into the hole.

"No, you move it," said a voice. "Don't hurt my babies," it said.

"Make your babies somewhere else, I need this spot to feed," retorted Tupac.

"Now come on, no fighting," said Carrie. Karen was so engrossed in watching Tupac feed that she didn't see Carrie come in. Carrie was near Tupac and with the light shining from Carrie, Karen saw a, tan and rod-shaped bacterium like Tupac and Buddy, except it was smaller than the two. It was Charlie. Charlie was resting against the mousse and next to it, were copy versions of it. Some were feeding on the mousse like Tupac. The Karen saw that one of the copy version of Charlie got wider and longer. A cleave form in the middle of its rod shape. The cleave got deeper and deeper, as if they would meet in the center. And they did and the rod-shape broke off into a half. The two halves were the same size Binary fission in action. They were all tan and rod-shaped with a single flagellum like Buddy and Tupac.

"Stop hurting my babies, Tupac," said Charlie. Charlie had a shivery voice.

"Go make babies somewhere else," retorted Tupac.

"No, I also need this food to feed and grow." Charlie was cut off by Tupac who said, "and to make babies."

"So what? Yeah, I make babies," Charlie got up and lashed its flagellum on Tupac. Tupac lashed its flagellum back. Flagellum fight.

"Stop it, you two!" yelled Buddy who ran over to stop the fight. "Now you both share this spot. It is liquidy, a good

feeding spot and plenty. Now share it," Buddy retorted.

"Hmm, looks good to me," Buddy continued on and anchored its flagellum into the hole in the mousse, the same location

where Tupac's flagellum was. Then Karen saw exactly what she saw with Tupac, Buddy was feeding by pinocytosis on

the dark liquid. "That was delicious food," said Buddy as it removed its flagellum and then came to a stop near Karen.

Near the holes, there were a lot of Charlies. Budding. The same way as Charlie. Each new generation will grow bigger, to Charlie's size. Then they would each split into two and each of the two split into two each and so on. They all looked flattened out and enlarged on the mousse when they split and then they fed, the same way that Tupac and Buddy fed, and after a while some of them moved around with their new flagellum. Karen noticed that a lot of creatures were swarming the surface of the mousse, feeding, growing, and undergoing binary fission. The light from Carrie caught Karen's attention to something else going on the surface of the mousse.

"Carrie, can you go around here?" Karen asked, pointing to an area with her fingers. And Carrie did. There was a lineup of Charlies at the surface of the mousse and below this line-up were layers and more layers of Charlie. This was a biofilm of Charlie. *Can there be others? Karen thought.*

Biofilm

A biofilm is a film that forms on a surface and is covered with microorganisms. They like to adhere to surfaces to feed and grow. In some biofilm, the growth is very thick. In a biofilm formation, microorganisms secrete exopolysaccharides that adhers to the surface. the exopolysaccharides allow the microorganisms to segregate together. Some microorganisms form a single layer while others form multi-layers in the exopolysaccharide secretion. Biofilms can be composed of populations of not always one type but also different types of organisms.

Karen looked carefully at the surface of the mousse. She saw a colorless outline surrounding the biofilm, like mucus attached to the surface of the mousse. *This might be the exopolysaccharides,* Karen thought. She saw a lot of places inside the mucus-like structure where the microorganisms were attached to the mousse in a layer and in some places, in multi-layers. There were colonies of microorganisms in several places in the mucus-like structure. Karen observed a diversity of shapes, sizes and color of microorganisms. Round, rod and spiral shapes. Polar flagella, some with flagella all over. White, yellow, tan, orange and brown colored ones. The same kinds were huddled together in many spots. Microorganisms in a biofilm do that. The same kinds in most cases huddle together.

Beanie burped. "This is delicious," it said. Karen looked curiously at Beanie. It wasn't feeding on the dark liquid that Karen saw others fed on.

It was feeding on a dead, decaying microorganism! A microorganism, dead or alive, is all organic. Its lopotrichous flagella were anchored in the mousse. A vesicle, filled with a watery looking substance, moved to the membrane inside Beanie. The vesicle fused with the membrane and the membrane bulged out with the cell wall. Beanie looked like it had a pimple there! The bulge kept getting bulgier until it looked almost like an O-shape attached to the cell wall. Then it pinched off and the waterylooking drop was outside of Beanie. This all happened by exocytosis. The watery-looking drop then moved toward the dead microorganism. The dead microorganism didn't look like any of the live microorganisms that Karen had seen. Its cell wall and membrane had ruptured and were scattered into pieces. Karen also pieces of some of the cell organelles, cytoplasm, nucleoid, flagella, all scattered around. The watery-looking drop touched a debris of the cell membrane that had lots of glycoprotein on it. The debris looked like it was melting. It started vanishing. Karen looked at it closely. It was still there, but as a greyish colored liquid surrounded by the watery-looking drop. The drop then moved to Beanie's cell wall. It fused and was taken in by endocytosis.

This was saprophytic feeding, feeding on dead and decaying matter. The processes for this feeding were endocytosis and exocytosis. The difference between Tupac's and Beanie's feeding was the food source. Tupac fed on the crude oil, the dark liquid, while Beanie fed on a dead microorganism The watery-looking drop consisted of enzymes that helped to break down the dead debris that Beanie took in.

"What were you feeding on, Beanie?" Karen asked. "Maggie," Beanie replied. "Maggie died a while back and I needed to dispose of it and so I fed on Maggie. Here Tupac, want some of Maggie?" Beanie asked.

"Nope, me like goo goo," replied Tupac as it rubbed against the dark liquid.

"Goo goo? Is that crude oil?" asked Karen. Tupac waved its flagellum, as if saying yes. "Well Karen, you appear lazy. All you have done during this visit is be fascinated by our feeding and defecation and reproduction. And I thought you were going to talk to me. ME!" retorted Buddy. There was silence.

"She hasn't seen all this before so closely. Don't forget Buddy that the first time you peered at Karen from the flask, you thought she was a zilla monster. And it took you a while to get comfortable with her," explained Carrie.

A zilla monster? Karen thought. That sounded funny to her.

"Alright, alright, I will be nice to your heroine, Carrie," Buddy grunted.

"Me love oil," squealed Tupac as it splashed on the blackish liquid. "This is yummy oil, Karen. Yummy. But we need more," wailed Tupac.

"More?" Karen asked. "There is so much of the mousse around you. That is more than plenty," she explained.

"How ignorant you are, Karen," Buddy chuckled. "Yes, there is a lot of mousse but only a small part of it is the edible oil that we can feed on," explained Buddy. "The rest of it is not edible for us even though it all looks dark colored. Do not be fooled by the color," Buddy continued explaining.

"But I thought you can break it down with the enzymes you have," explained Karen.

"Nope. We can't feed on most of the mousse. That's why our kinds are dying " said Buddy, sounding sad. "Rico and its gang secretes that chemical that helps them to eat most of the mousse but that same chemical also kills us," explained Buddy.

"Something for me to look into," thought Karen. "I'd love to observe how Rico and its gang does that," said Karen.

They all felt something move by. "Rico is around," Tupac whispered and then hid behind Buddy.

"Let's get you out of the flask before Rico does something," continued Buddy.

Karen had forgotten all about coming into the flask. It felt like she has been in the flask for ages. She had forgotten all about her human world until Buddy reminded her just now. *How long had she been there? What time was it? Andy must be worried, she thought.* What if they called the police and reported her missing? What if there were sniffer dogs in the lab, trying to get hints of Karen's disappearance? Maybe sniffing at the flask and what if it breaks and all her microbuddies die? *I have never heard of sniffer dogs in the lab. That can't be,* Karen said to herself. At this point, both her human world and the flask held special for her. She was going to miss the micro-buddies, she could already feel it.

"I guess I should get going, Buddy. I am worried about Andy and others," said Karen.

"Who is Andy, huh?" asked Buddy and whipped its flagellum on Karen's face.

"My boyfriend," explained Karen.

"Boyfriend? You have a boyfriend?" asked Buddy surprised.

"So?" retorted back Karen.

"What is it like?" asked Buddy.

"Like a human," answered Carrie.

"I didn't ask you, Carrie," yelled Buddy.

"Sorrry, so much interest in her boyfriend," Carrie replied back sarcastically.

"He is handsome, lovable and my soulmate," replied Karen softly, out of missing Andy.

"And me? I don't mean anything to you, do I?" yelled Buddy.

"No you do! You do, Buddy! You all are my friends. I feel so good to have been in the flask. I felt so good spending time with you all. I want you to be my micro-buddies. I want to keep visiting you and spending time with you," explained Karen.

"That was very touching. It is a pleasure for us to have you as OUR buddy too," said Buddy.

"Yay!" came a big roar.

"We like you, Karen," said Carrie.

"Sweet Karen. You are my friend," said Tupac as it gently whipped it flagellum in Karen's face. Karen laughed, they were sweet.

"So when are we going to see you again, Karen?" asked Buddy.

"In a few days. I need to find out how long I was here and what day it is. You see, humans have schedules. I have lab work, I need to talk to Dr. Rogers about my work progress, I need to finish off a paper, I need spend time with Andy, I need to go to the gym, I need to call my sister…" Karen said and was cut off by Buddy who said, "that's a lot to do. But do you have to do all this?" asked Buddy.

"Of course I do. My lab work is supported by a grant that supports my personal expenses, Dr. Rogers is my advisor and I need to make progress in my work or I can't renew my grant or possibly not get new grants in the future, Andy is my love, my sister is my emotional support," replied Karen.

"And we?" retorted Buddy.

"You are my micro-buddies. Without you all, I won't understand my lab work. You make my world easier," said Karen.

"That feels nice," Buddy said. They were on the edge of the flask. "So I guess it is good bye now," said Buddy, sounding sad.

"Yes. BUT I will be back, I promise," replied Karen and rubbed her hands against the flask and she got swooshed out.

A few days later, Karen sat in her office thinking what she saw on her last trip to the flask. She had analyzed all the samples she got with the help from the micro-buddies during her visit in the flask. The microorganisms with the light in them were *Vibrio fischerii* strains. She was able to observe their behavior under the light microscope. Symbiotic microorganisms. She also took some fresh samples, scooped from the flask, for confirmation and they were there. And DNA analyses from the samples confirmed that they were *Vibrio fischerii* strains. The mousse was crude oil and she was able to confirm that by running the sample of it using gas chromatography mass spectrometry. While she was in the flask, Carrie gave her a smear of Rico and Rico's babies. The smear was more than 90% related to *Mycobacterium vanbaleeniii*. So, Buddy and its gang ran away from Rico and its gang which were a strain of *Mycobacterium vanbaleeniii*. They can be killed by some antibiotics but they also secreted a chemical that Buddy said could kill them and that's why they were running away from it. The microbes formed a biofilm on the crude oil's surface. She still needed to take samples from the chemical secretion from Rico and its gangs and that red rock. What a world out there! Karen thought. Friends, foes, competition for food and space. Interactions just like in the human world!

Chapter 4

The Killers

Karen looked at the spectrophotometer absorbance reading for the cellular proteins from the flask that contained the micro-buddies. She had taken an aliquot of the culture from the flask, centrifuged it thrice at 6000 rpm for 15 minutes to pellet the cells, each time discarding the supernatant and re-suspending the cell pellet in crude-oil free Bushnell Haas medium, because that was the medium in the culture flask. Then she lysed the suspended cell pellet and centrifuged it again and used the supernatant in the protein assay for which she used the spectrophotometer.

The cellular protein concentration was going down over days. It was now 10% lower than what she had observed and recorded last week. That was a faster rate of decrease than she had observed before. The cellular protein measurement gives the amount of total protein in the culture aliquot and is representative of cell density and growth. A high cellular protein value means that there are a lot of proteins in the cells, which means there are a lot of cells. An increase in the cellular protein value means that there is an increase in cell density, which in turn means that there are more live cells than dead cells and that the culture is growing.

The low cellular protein concentration implied that the micro-buddies were dying. Could Rico and its gang be on a killing rampage? It had been two weeks since Karen visited the flask. She had been immersed in writing a research manuscript. What Karen thought would take a week extended into two weeks. At least she hadn't announced her anticipated deadline for handing in the manuscript to Dr. Rogers. Karen learned from experience that writing manuscripts can take unexpected, over the schedule time. Karen remembered her first manuscript. She had thought she would be done in about a week and even drafted up a schedule for doing the different sections for the manuscript. AND she told Dr. Rogers that she would hand in her manuscript the following week. The weekend before her announced deadline, Karen stayed up the whole night on Saturday but was unable to go on at her expected speed and state of thinking. Andy came over to her desk early in the morning and lovingly put his arms around Karen.

"Come on, baby, let's go to bed. You can do it tomorrow morning," he said. But Karen would have none of it. It had to be done because she was embarrassed that she told Dr. Rogers that she would hand in the paper on Monday. Unable to think any more, Karen went to bed, hoping to speed up the next morning. When she woke up, it was afternoon! She jumped out of bed, flew into a rage, looking for Andy to blow up on. Andy was nowhere to be found. Karen saw a note on the bathroom's mirror saying that he was off to get groceries and that he left some hot coffee for her. That evening, Karen was still on the computer and then realized that she was still only halfway through the paper and there was no way she could finish it that night. She was looking pale and tired. Andy persuaded her to take a break. The next day, she nervously went to Dr. Rogers' office and when she told her the situation, Dr. Rogers warmly explained to her that she understood and it was all ok. She wished Karen good luck on the paper, gave her a hug and then asked her to join her for lunch. During lunch, they laughed about Dr. Rogers' first few experiences in writing manuscripts. Karen was indeed lucky to have such a kind, understanding and extremely supportive advisor. However, that was not the first and last experience with unrealistic deadlines. It happened a second time but that time, Karen gave herself an extra week before announcing to Dr. Rogers about her submission deadline. When that extra one week arrived, Karen thought she could take it easy and still be done. She soaked up on internet celebrity gossip and hardly made progress on her paper. Then in the last remaining days, she forced herself to speed up on the paper.

She ended up feeling tired. By the end of that week, Karen was still not done. Then slowly over time, Karen learned the ropes of steady writing for manuscripts and got the feel of what was involved and how to spread and stretch out her writing schedule. She learned how to balance writing time with some "me" time.

This time, Karen was done in time and had proudly handed in her manuscript to Dr. Rogers. Dr. Rogers had this tradition of giving students their favorite candy bar whenever they submit written work to her. She knew the favorite candy bars for all her students and kept stacks of them with her. Karen got hers this time, Monster Chew.

It was time to go see Buddy, Tupac and the others. Using her right palm, she made three downward strokes on the flask- the magic rub- and got whisked in.

"Buddy?" she called out as she floated in darkness.

"Karen!" came Buddy's voice and she felt the flagellum next to her hands. She grasped it. "Karen! Good old, Karen.

You are back!" said Buddy with excitement.

"Of course, I am back. I missed you all," said Karen.

"Really?" asked Buddy, as it quickly pulled away the flagellum from her. "You missed us?" Buddy continued while it playfully whipped its flagellum on Karen's face. "You missed this whipping? Did you?" continued Buddy playfully. Then Karen felt more whipping, this time from another flagellum.

"He, he, he, hi, Karen," it went. It was Tupac. Both were whipping her playfully. She did miss them. Then Tupac did the unexpected, it tickled her tummy with its flagellum.

Karen started giggling and then grasped Tupac's flagellum. "Stop it!" she said. "Why? This is fun," said Tupac while tugging on its flagellum to get it freed from Karen's grip. "Please, Tupac. No more whipping," pleaded Karen.

"I am not doing it no more, Karen," Tupac whined. "It is Buddy. Let go of my tail. I don't want it broken. Go grab

Buddy's tail. Not mine."

"Why?" asked Buddy mockingly.

"Because I am cute," replied Tupac assertively.

"Yes, you are cute, Tupac. But tugging your tail away from Karen makes you a wimp," Buddy said teasingly.

Then all of a sudden, Tupac took off with Karen. Full speed. And Karen felt like flying. She felt nauseous.

"Slow down, Tupac. Slow down," Buddy yelled. Buddy was racing behind Tupac.

"Yeah, Karen and I," said Tupac excitedly. And it kept zooming at full speed."I am going to show you lots of stuff," said Tupac. Suddenly, there was a big rock-like structure in front of them. Tupac bumped into it. DONK! It hit Karen's head. Karen was in shock and she let go of Tupac's flagellum. She was floating. And scared. And nauseous. AND her head was hurting a bit from the rock-bumping.

Tupac thought Karen was still holding its flagellum. "Wowwwww!" yelled Tupac as it continued speeding.

"Karen?" she heard Buddy calling. Karen was massaging her head and also trying to catch her breath.

"Hey, Karen. You ok, Karen?" Buddy was hovering around her and gently stroking her forehead with its flagellum. By now, Tupac realized that Karen wasn't riding with it, made a U-turn and was approaching Karen and Buddy. "Look what you did to her, Tupac. Bad, Tupac. Sure, it didn't hurt you. But she is human and they hurt," yelled Buddy at Tupac.

"Sorry. I was just trying to have fun with her," said Tupac in a squeaky voice.

"You and your fun," yelled Buddy. "Karen?" asked Buddy again, sounding concerned. "Karen, are you- " and before Buddy could continue, Karen grabbed Buddy's flagellum.

"Yes, I am ok. Just a little breathless and nauseous."

"See, Tupac, you made her feel sick," yelled Buddy.

"I am sorrrry," said Tupac. "I was trying to have a fun ride with her. I am sorry, pleeease," begged Tupac.

"That's OK, Tupac. I don't mind. I am OK now," explained Karen as she held on to Buddy's flagellum. "Sweet Karen," Tupac lovingly lashed its flagellum on Karen.

Karen wondered what that red rock was. She was guessing that it might be the ferric chloride that she had added into the medium in the flask. It looked bright red, just the color of ferric chloride. She had added a pinch of this only in the medium and because it was not too much that she added, that's probably why it was her second encounter only with this rock. So presumably, it was ferric chloride, she thought to herself. *There might be a bit on my head and I might be able to use that*, Karen thought.

What if I tell them that I am not OK?, Karen thought. She decided to act insomniac.

"Oh, my head," she moaned. "I can't think. It is all blank. Oooohhhhh," she continued moaning.

"Karen!!!" Tupac squeaked louder and kept tapping its flagellum on her head. It didn't hurt but it tickled. "Karen, don't dieeeee!!!" yelled Tupac and this time, started to brush its body on Karen's head. Ugh! It smelled strongly of soil. Like she was immersed in soil and walking in it. Tupac was now brushing its flagellum over Karen's head. It was very ticklish and Karen tried not to giggle and to act braindamaged.

"Stop it, Tupac. Stop rubbing your tail on her head!" yelled Buddy.

"I didn't mean to kill her, Buddy. I didn't," wailed Tupac.

Karen didn't move.

"Karen, can you see me?" asked Buddy.

"Where are you?" lied Karen. She acted blind by moving her hands around.

"Oh my God! She is blind," said Buddy.

"And also dumb," added Tupac in a little voice. They both stood still, looking at her.

Then Buddy said, "Maybe Alex can help."

Alex? Who is Alex and what will it do? Karen wondered. "Hee hee heee heee, hee hee hee," Tupac kept giggling and giggling.

"Come on, Tupac," snapped Buddy.

"Alex is a clown," said Tupac.

"Will you go and get Alex?" yelled Buddy.

"OK," replied Tupac wearily and swam off.

"And get Bernie if you can, Tupac" yelled Buddy in Tupac's direction.

Buddy put its flagellum in Karen's hands and she held it firmly. Hopefully, Buddy wouldn't doubt if she was lying. She intended to keep up with the game as far as she could to see what was happening. Buddy gently stroked her forehead with its soily-smelling, gooey-covered body. It was stinky.

But Karen didn't want to offend Buddy.

"Who is Alex and what will it do?" asked Karen.

"Alex is a medicine guy," replied Buddy. "He has magic power to help us. Alex will help you too, hopefully. Oh Karen, I am so sorry!" said Buddy, sounding sad. "I am so sorry to let Tupac take you for a ride. Tupac didn't mean to hurt you, it is just naive and excited to take you for a ride," explained Buddy, all the while gently rubbing her forehead with its stinky body.

"Buddy?" asked Karen. "Buddy, can you take me for a gentle ride? Just a slow ride," Karen asked, only because she wanted the rubbing on her to stop. She couldn't take the stinky smell no more.

"Sure," replied Buddy and took her on a slow motion ride. "How is that?" it asked.

"That makes me feel better," replied Karen promptly. It did make her feel better. In slow motion they went and in darkness all around.

Then Karen saw a glimmer of light. It got stronger and bigger. And then she recognized it. It was Bernie. And with Bernie was Tupac and a strange looking thing. It was colorless and had many noodles coming out of a thin stem and with bumps on the ends of the noodles. The thin stem was attached at its bottom to a white looking crystal. Without Bernie's light, Karen would not have seen this creature.

"You OK, Karen?" Bernie asked.

"Yes, she is OK. But I guess blind and blank," replied Buddy. "Did I describe your symptoms right, Karen?" asked Buddy. Karen nodded her head.

"She is mute now," exclaimed Tupac. "And dumb," it whispered.

"No, I am not mute," snapped Karen.

"Come on, Tupac, be good now. Or I will send you to Rico!" yelled Buddy. "It is all my fault. If only I didn't let you take Karen for a ride, this wouldn't have happen," exclaimed Buddy. "Karen is our savior and our best friend. Only she can make life interesting for us and also save us from starvation. And from Rico," said Buddy.

"And Rico's gang," added Bernie.

"I don't want to go to Rico!" whimpered Tupac.

"OK, calm down," added Karen. "Tupac, you won't be sent to Rico," said Karen.

"See how nice she is. Now, Tupac, you will behave yourself!" demanded Buddy.

"I will behave myself," said Tupac in a squeaky voice. "What? Say it again, louder and slower," said Buddy. "I WILL BEHAVE MYSELF," yelled Tupac.

"Good," added Bernie. "Now Alex, can you help?" "What are the symptoms?" Alex asked.

"Blind, blank," replied Buddy.

"Well, I am not sure if I can help with my secretion. It is to help make your gangs get and stay strong but as you know, it cannot keep you from dying from exposure to Rico and its gang's secretions," explained Alex. Karen was terrified. What was it going to do to her? What was in its secretion?

"Well, try your secretion," said Buddy. "That's the best hope we have. Karen is OUR hope for survival. And she needs her eyes and brain to help us," explained Buddy. Karen gulped. What was going to happen?

"The good news is that I am starving. Which means that I can make lots of those medical secretions," said Alex happily.

"I see that! Your food reserve is a tiny peck," said Buddy and went near the white crystal on which Alex was based. So that white crystal was Alex's food! Karen was enamored by Alex. It was like no other. It can't be a bacterium. Then it occurred to Karen! Alex was a fungus. Yes, a fungus! And that explained it all. The long horizontal stem that looked like pieces glued together were septate hyphae. A collection of them formed the mycelium. The vertical stems coming out of the hyphae were conidiophores. Out of these shorter sac-like branches called phialides came the white crystal which might be the sugar source. Fungi are not free-motile organisms, like bacteria. They are anchored to a food source or a support. *Oh well*, Karen thought, *I can get a sample of that too before I leave.*

Karen noticed vesicles moving in some of Alex's hyphae, and Alex was standing real close to Karen's forehead. Then the colorless liquid from the vesicle moved out of the hyphae. Probably by diffusion. Karen had not seen a close up of chemical secretion from fungi and this was the first observation for her, thanks to the light from Bernie or she would have been in complete darkness and not seen what she just saw. Alex pushed the liquid toward Karen by swimming around. What was that liquid? What would it do to her? Karen's heart started pounding. She jerked away from the colorless liquid moving towards her. holding Buddy's flagellum

"Noooo! Get that away from me!" she yelled.

"Are you OK?" asked Buddy.

"Yeah, I am OK now," she replied.

"But please, don't let that liquid from Alex touch me," she wailed. She was eyeing the liquid moving near her and she was trying to keep it from touching her while also holding Buddy's flagellum.

"So you can see the medical secretion?" asked Buddy. "Of course, I see the medical secretion and I don't want it to touch me. I will die," yelled Karen.

"So you can see?" asked Buddy.

"Can you please get me away from this secretion? Please?," wailed Karen.

"Excuse me! I thought this creature needed my help, Buddy," exclaimed Alex.

Oh well…that's what I thought," replied Buddy. It was now moving away from the secretion with Karen holding on its flagellum. Everyone else was following.

"This took me a lot of energy to produce," Alex exclaimed.

"I'm so sorry, Alex. I understand. I appreciate you helping Karen. I thought she needed help," explained Buddy.

"Apology accepted. I have an appointment with Julie. I better go," replied Alex and went away.

Buddy then turned to Karen and said, "How can you see all of a sudden? Magic?" "You were fooling around?" Karen gulped. It was not funny for her anymore.

"You were kidding all along. My head! My eyes! Liar," retorted Buddy. By now, Bernie and Carrie were there.

"WHY?" yelled Buddy. "And I believed you!" Buddy said, feeling hurt.

"You have no idea how bad Alex feels. And get this in your head right now: Alex is a VERY important part of our world. We break Alex's trust, we all die," exclaimed Buddy.

Buddy was slowly sliding its flagellum away from Karen's grip.

"I am sorry," Karen said and firmed her grasp on Buddy's flagellum. "I was just trying to have a little fun. I mean, it was so cute the way Tupac took me for a ride. And then I bonked on that red thing. And I decided to get into the acting mode to see what you guys would do if I was hurt," explained Karen, still holding onto Buddy's flagellum firmly. "So I am sorry. I truly feel sorry for Alex. But I am also truly touched, touched from my heart, the way you all took care of me, including how Alex tried taking care of me. Now I know and I believe that you all will take care of me if I get hurt in this flask," continued Karen.

"Or even if you die in this flask," Bernie added.

"Just don't eat my decomposed body," said Karen in a little voice. She could imagine Bernie eating her dead body just like she saw Beanie saprophytically feeding on Maggie's corpse the other day.

"I will make sure about that," said Buddy reassuringly. "We will take care of you," it continued. "Well, just send me out of the flask in that case," explained Karen.

"We can take care of you," asserted Buddy. There was silence. So they would try to take care of her in the flask if she was sick or dead. For how long? What about Andy? He would worry about her. She would need to stay with Buddy to avoid an accident and to build a trusting friendship. But what if she couldn't get in the flask if she is ever sick? *Give Buddy a chance*, she said to herself. Maybe Carrie would help. Carrie was the most loving in the group. "Thanks, Buddy," Karen said.

There was dead silence for a moment.

Then Bernie asked, " How are you holding up, Buddy? You are looking weak. We have to find a way to help us," said Bernie.

"You are starving, Buddy? What's going on? I knew it! That's why I came back," chipped in Karen. "I saw that the growth rate was decreasing for your world. And that's why I came back," continued Karen.

"Rosie died. Also Kate. And then there is John, Rob…." said Buddy.

"How many died lately?" asked Karen.

"We can't keep track of the numbers. But in masses," replied Buddy.

"We are going to die, I don't want to die. Noooo," Tupac started wailing.

"No one will die, Tupac. Now come on, stop wailing. We don't have time. I need information and then action," said Karen.

Buddy told Karen about Rico and its gang. They were finishing off the black mousse, leaving inedible parts that Buddy and others couldn't eat. Rico and its gang could eat the inedible part after emulsifying it with a killer chemical that they produced but that could also kill Buddy's gang. The more they feasted on the black mousse, the more they grew in number, the more of this killer chemical they produced and the more of Buddy's members died.

"The black mousse is the oil," Karen explained. "And Rico and its gang are scientifically called *Mycobacterium vanbaleeniii*," Karen told them, sounding pleased.

"What can they do?" asked Buddy.

"I don't know. All I know is that they are commonly found at oil sites and that they can be killed by some antibiotics," she replied. Her thoughts were on Alex and its secretion. *Was it antibiotics that Alex secreted?*, Karen thought. Even if it was, then Rico and its gang were probably resistant to it or by now, they would be killed.

They all went towards the oil and as they got near to it, Bernie and its kind left them in the darkness out of politeness so that Buddy and the rest would not be seen by Rico and its gang. They went into a little groove in the oil mousse, like the one they were in last time when they were running away from Rico's gang. It was dark. They went a little deeper into the groove. There was a light shining. It was Beanie.

"Hello. A lot for me to feed on today," greeted Beanie. There were a lot of corpses, some shriveled and some disintegrated. The shriveled ones were probably the fresh kills and they still had their shapes, some round, some rodshaped, and some irregular shapes. Karen didn't see any spiral shapes among the corpses. Beanie went back to feeding, the same way Karen had observed last time- saprophytic feeding using exo- and endocytosis mechanisms, i.e. by joining Beanie were a lot of other strains of *Vibrio fischerii*.

"Shh, look out. But quietly," whispered Buddy. Karen ducked her head out of the groove quietly and looked in the direction that Tupac pointed with its flagellum.

"Thank you, Tupac," Buddy whispered.

"Tupac, will you give me a hand to move this?" Beanie asked and Tupac disappeared.

"Look in front of you," Buddy said.

Karen saw a light. It was Joey. Joey was feeding on a dead microorganism. BUT a few feet away from Joey, near the oil mousse, was Rico and its gang. They were feeding on the oil mousse by exocytosis and endocytosis. She was wondering what that chemical was that they secreted in exocytosis that helped to solubilize some of the oil in it and the solubilized mixture was then taken in by endocytosis. She had to find a way to get a sample of that secreted chemical.

Rico and its gang kept eating the oil mousse and then Karen saw that some of them also took a short break and were budding off. They were growing in number by binary fission. The blackish-brownish oil mousse was disappearing rapidly and what was left behind was a blackish tarred-like solid chunk. Small, looked smooth, irregular shaped but shiny. Like the tar resulting from combustion. Joey was standing next to Rico, all the while Karen was observing Rico feed. It helped her visibly see what was going on. "What are you going to do with it, Joey?" asked Rico. "No one can eat that."

"Nothing, just helping you get it out of the way," replied Joey. Rico kept eating fresh oil mousse while Joey flapped its lipotrichous flagella to make the inedible tarry-looking chunk move towards where Buddy and Karen were hiding. Joey kept moving slowly to the hole where

Karen and Buddy were hiding and kept flapping its flagellum to get the chunk near the hole. When it did, Buddy grabbed it for Karen to feel and Joey went away, interested in eating more decomposed bodies. The tarry-looking chunk was solid, black in color, and sticky. It strongly reeked of crude oil.

"We can't eat this," Buddy said, sounding regretful. Karen took a chunk of it and slipped it into a small vial in her lab coat. She had also taken more samples of others that she needed, including from Alex. And yes, she still had a bit of the red rock powder on her forehead.

Rico was still feeding in that spot and even if they got close to him, the secretion bubbling off from Rico and its nearby gang members, would kill Buddy and its species on contact. So having the secretion wave towards them would not work. She would need to keep Buddy and Tupac away from Rico and its secretion. She had an idea. Beanie was still inside the cave where they were, feeding on the dead mass.

"Beanie, can you do me a favor?" Karen asked. Beanie kept feeding.

"Greedy Beanie," muttered Buddy.

"Beanie needs a treat, Karen," Tupac said exasperatedly, "or it doesn't care or listen." Karen thought of a way to get to Beanie. "Beanie, how about some poop?" Karen asked.

"What kind of poop?" Beanie looked up and asked.

"Ummm, how about mine?" Karen asked, feeling weird. Tupac started laughing but softens its sound, out of fear that Rico might hear them.

"That's disgusting, Karen," Buddy replied.

"That's… that's ew." Beanie looked up and said, "sorry, me don't eat poop. Me need something dead and decomposing."

Karen raced in her thoughts. Something dead and decomposing. Hmmmm… She thought about the ocean.

"How about a squid?"

"What??????" Buddy asked. "You crazy? A squid will ingest us. We will die," explained Buddy.

"We will die…" wailed Tupac who had been with Beanie all the while.

"Shhhhh" cut off Buddy. "No, no, Tupac. Come here to me. No one will die," Buddy said as Tupac came near to it and Buddy caressed it with its body. If Tupac wailed about dying, the sound would have been audible to Rico and then they would all be on the run from Rico and its gang. So Buddy tried soothing Tupac.

"How about a piece of rotten fish?" asked Karen.

"That would be good!" replied Beanie.

"Karen, do you know what you are doing?" asked Buddy angrily. "Where are you going to get this stuff from? And even if you get it, you will make the situation worse," Buddy added. "You will introduce micro-aliens along with the rotten

fish to the flask and what if they kill us?"

Buddy had a point. All living things and even non-living things harbor microorganisms on the surface and in them. The dead piece of fish might contain a lot of *Vibrio fischerii* of different strains or subspecies or other microorganisms. And they might not get along with the ones living in this flask. They might compete and even outcompete Buddy, Beanie, and others.

"Ok, how about this Beanie?" Buddy asked. "How about if we take you to more dead bodies to feed on?"

That was a good idea and simple too, Karen thought.

Wow! Buddy was smart! Smarter than Karen!

"Yeah," Beanie said immediately. "That will work. Take me to more dead bodies."

"Ok, then we will. But you know that you need to do something for us too, right?" asked Buddy. Beanie nodded its lopotrichous flagella.

"Karen, what is it that you want to negotiate with Beanie?" asked Buddy.

"How about if you find Beanie some dead bodies first? Then you come back to Tupac and I while Beanie can take Rico and its gang to feast on the top of this mousse Beanie can then flap its flagella to make Rico's secretion move towards us. You and Tupac hide deep in this cave so that the secretion doesn't touch you. I can remain with you, but near the cave's entrance to collect the secretion. And then when I am done, Beanie can take Rico and its gang somewhere else so that I can get out of this flask and work on finding a solution for you. And while I am gone, get Beanie some more dead bodies to feast on," Karen explained.

They all agreed, even Beanie. Karen reminded Beanie to stay away from the secretion, to not let it touch it, but to flap its flagella so that is moves in her direction.

"I will need lots of dead bodies," Beanie said.

"Oh yes. There are a few right now in this hole. Why don't you finish eating these first?" Buddy answered.

After Beanie finished eating, Karen, Buddy and Tupac huddled in the cave. Buddy and Tupac moved in deeper. Beanie, satisfied with its appetite, then approached Rico.

Rico and its gang were feeding on another mousse a few feet away from where they were before.

"What's up Beanie?" Rico asked.

"How is it going?" Beanie asked.

"Busy eating. This is like heaven. No Buddy and Tupac or any of their kinds. Soon, they will be extinct," Rico laughed.

"Looks like that time IS near. There are a lot of dead bodies in that cave for me to eat, thanks to you Rico. And Rico, the mousse on top of this cave looks so yummy. You might want to see it," Beanie continued. "Come on, follow me friends. I owe you this for all the dead bodies you gave me to eat," Beanie said.

"Oh, we are buddies. I eat the slick, make dead bodies and you eat the dead bodies," exclaimed Rico.

Proudly. Beanie took them to a spot on the top of mousse, while Karen, Buddy, and Tupac remained hidden in the nearby cave. "Hey, Rico, try this. This is foamy," Beanie said.

"Yummy!" Rico said.

"There are some dead bodies here," Rico pointed to Beanie. Beanie started to feast on the bodies while Rico and one of its gang members, Judy, fed on top of the cave. Rico secreted this colorless bubble by exocytosis. The bubble landed on the dense mousse and that part of the mousse got solubilized. It was like removing dirt from a t-shirt using detergent, the bubbly colorless chemical the equivalent of a detergent here. The solubilized mousse part was taking in by Rico by endocytosis.

"Hmm, delicious" exclaimed Rico. There were more of the colorless, bubbly chemical secretion floating all around and Beanie waved its lipotrichous flagella to get some of the colorless, bubbly chemical go downward to the cave. It didn't want to touch it or it would die too. "Good way to kill any of Buddy gang members alive in the cave, Beanie," Rico laughed off. Beanie kept flagging the chemical secretion towards the entrance of the cave by moving its flagella in a rhythm.

Inside, right at the entrance, Karen opened a vial she was carrying and scooped up some of the chemical. Buddy and Tupac had huddled in deeper with Buddy's flagellum around Karen's waist. She didn't want to float off. She quickly closed the vial and looked at Buddy who pulled her in.

"Hey, hold on to this or you will float off," Buddy exclaimed. Karen quickly grabbed the flagellum. Wow! She was very close to being drifted out of the cave. Outside was Beanie and when it saw Karen move in deeper, it moved away from that place. Beanie was busy feeding nearby the hole where they were hiding.

Then suddenly, Beanie appeared near them and demanded "I need dead bodies right now. Where are my dead bodies?"

"Beanie, we need to fend off from this chemical coming near us and then we will take you to dead bodies," explained Buddy.

"Nope, need dead bodies now," it exclaimed. The colorless, bubbly chemical was moving towards them. It was like a big foam of bubbles and there was no way around it for them to move. It kept drifting towards them. Up there, Rico and its gang were busy feeding on the foamy mousse.

Suddenly Charlie, a member of Buddy's gang, appeared at the hole where the group was hiding. It had made its way from the bottom of the mousse. Karen gasped as she saw what started happening to Charlie. She moved forward, trying to wave the chemical away from Charlie but it was too late. Charlie, who was Buddy's kind of microorganism, started becoming distorted. The chemical secretion kept moving quickly to the rest of Charlie, engulfing it, distorting it and releasing its organelles into space. Charlie was gone, dead. Karen stood stunned. She sucked in her breath. She couldn't scream or Rico might hear it. She started sobbing at what she saw.

"Oh wow! This looks good," Beanie said and started to feast on dead Charlie.

"Here, hold on to it," Buddy said helplessly. Tupac started sobbing and so did Karen. And the bubbly chemical was moving towards them. Nearer and nearer. Beanie was done too soon.

Rico heard the sobs and looked in the hole.

"MOVE!" yelled Karen. She yelled so loud that Buddy zoomed off from the cave with Karen zooming off, holding tightly onto Buddy's flagellum. In a flash, they swiftly got out of the hole, just in time before the chemical secretion got to them.

Rico and Judy followed them. Then others from their gang joined Rico. But Karen, Buddy and Rico were not alone. They were joined by Carrie, Bernie and others and the light from them helped Karen to see in the darkness. There were so many of the mousse caves, so many of the hard, inedible chunks, so many of the red rocks. There were more of Rico's look-alikes, yellow, rod-shapes, feeding on the mousse and the colorless, bubbly secretions around them.

There were masses of dead microorganisms, all disintegrated with floating organelles, a few floating around near the mousse and some piled up in the holes in the mousse.

"Oh my goodness," Alex yelled and moved along with them. There were more of Alex lookalikes. Long thin colorless hyphae with a white base attached to them. So now they had a sizeable number following them- Bernie's group and Alex's group AND also a lot of Buddy's group. Behind them was Rico's group. There was a big red rock in front of them. As they got near it, Karen flung it back with her feet in an attempt to hurl it at Rico. Rico's group swiftly moved above the rock and kept moving.

"You think the rock will hit them? What a idiot you are, Karen!" Buddy exclaimed as they kept moving. Karen did feel like an idiot. These microorganisms could easily and swiftly move in any directions with the help of their strong, muscular flagella. And a rock was not going to hit them.

They would move away from it.

"How about going in a cave, Buddy?" Karen pleaded.

"Calm down, Karen. Calm down. You know what happened in the cave. This time, Rico will come in," Buddy explained. Buddy was right. Karen was petrified and acting like an idiot.

Alex and its group started secreting their colorless medicine chemical. It swam towards Rico and its gang.

"Come on, secrete more!" commanded Alex.

"It doesn't do anything to them. Nothing. And it takes energy to make all this," yelled another Alex lookalike, but taller than Alex.

"I know, Julie, but it is better than nothing," replied Alex.

"That makes no sense, I am not doing it anymore unless it is for a different cause," replied Julie. "Be reasonable, Alex," Julie added.

"Bernie, you and your people need to go away. Your light helps them follow us," yelled Buddy.

"But we are just trying to help you," replied Bernie.

"Please go and distract Rico and its gang, will you?" yelled Buddy. "I haven't eaten in days and I am getting tired of this movement," continued Buddy.

"Me too," replied Tupac.

"How far away are we from the side of the flask?" Karen asked.

"The side of the flask is the favorite place for Rico to feed on. There is a lot of mousse stuck there," replied Buddy.

"Ok, we will leave you guys and try to coax Rico and its gang," replied Bernie.

"Thanks, Bernie and group," replied Buddy and they kept moving forward, it got darker as saw Bernie and its group went away. Rico and its gang avoided Bernie and the group and kept coming after them.

"I am going to die, I better go," replied Alex.

"Yeah, better to go and get some rest, Alex. Thank you for trying to help us," replied Buddy.

"You are welcome, Buddy, Tupac, and Karen. Please take care of us all, Karen" said Alex.

"I will, I promise," replied Karen. So now there were just the three of them, Buddy, Tupac and Karen, and behind them were Rico and its gang.

Karen could feel Buddy and Tupac slowing down. Buddy's flagellum was propelling weakly. And Rico and its gang were getting closer. Karen could see Rico clearly now. Yellow, smooth, rod shaped. But interestingly, no flagellum! It moved by propelling its body forward. Karen identified Rico as a *Mycobacterium vanbaleenii* strain based on the smear that she took for some of its members. She better take another sample. And this time, a smear of Rico's current baby generation. *M. vanbaleenii* responds to some of the antibiotics and yes, flagella have not been observed with this species, but they are non-motile. So either Rico was a different species, not the sample she took, or a different subspecies or strain of *M. vanbaleenii*.

There was a big mousse cave ahead of them. And there was white light getting brighter as they moved ahead, which meant that they were getting near the side of the flask. But Buddy's speed was slowing down. It was tired.

"Buddy, let's get in the cave. Come on," Karen said. "Rico will get there," it said tiredly.

"Buddy, we will deal with it. I will distract Rico and then

get out of the flask. Meanwhile, you and Tupac go and hide. I will distract Rico with the mousse," Karen said.

"But the secretion from Rico might kill you too," Buddy replied.

"I will take care of that. AND I promise I will come back and help you. We got to do this, Buddy. Come on. Let's get in the cave," Karen pleaded.

"Please, Buddy, let's get in the cave. I am tired. I am dying," wailed Tupac.

They dived into the mousse cave. Rico and gang followed. They crawled in deeper and deeper.

"Tupac, go in deeper and rest," Buddy said.

"Bye, Karen. Please come back," said Tupac in its trademark squeaky voice.

"I will, promise. Now go," Karen replied.

"Now if we go in deeper, you might have a hard time getting out," said Buddy.

"Buddy, go. I can get on top of the mousse and rub the flask and leave," Karen said. "I am sure. Come on, Buddy. I will come back. Promise. I will help you find a way to also eat the oil and not get killed by Rico," she explained and let go of Buddy's flagellum.

"OK," Buddy gave in. Buddy crawled in deeper. Karen turned around. There was Rico, standing.

"What are you?" asked Rico.

"Me?" asked Karen. Rico had a husky voice. It came near her and then went up, down and around in a circle. "I... I am Karen," she said.

"Well, what kind are you? You are not a microorganism.

And you don't smell edible," said Rico.

"I am a human," said Karen.

"What the hell are you doing here, human Karen?" demanded Judy, another of Rico's kind but significantly bigger than Rico.

"Ummm, I came for a visit," she said.

"A visit or an adventure?" asked Rico.

"Both," Karen said. "But I will leave soon and won't bother you," she said.

"Leave? Where did you come from?" asked Raymond, another of their kind but this one smaller than Rico. "Outside," replied Karen. "Outside from the flask," she said.

"You mean from where the light is coming from?" asked Rico.

"Yes," replied Karen promptly. Her heart beat slowed down, she was not that freaked out as she was when she first met Rico. "How about if you take me up there? There is yummy mousse and you can eat that while I also show you the world outside the flask?" asked Karen.

"Buddy is in there, right?" said Rico. "Buddy ate that mousse cake. That cake was one of its kind. And I am not going to leave Buddy alive," Rico demanded. Karen's heart started pounding again.

"The mousse up there is delicious. I will pluck some for you to eat it. And I don't know if you know it but I feed this flask with the crude oil," said Karen.

"What is that?" asked Judy.

"That is the mousse that you eat," explained Karen. "When I go out of the flask, I will make sure to put in fresh crude oil so that you can eat it."

"So you have been getting in and out of the flask?" asked Rico.

"Yes," said Karen.

"AND helping Buddy escape!" yelled Rico.

"No, Buddy never escaped. Buddy is my friend," she yelled back. "But so are you," she softened up. Karen knew she had to play around to buy time to distract Rico and its gang so that Buddy and Tupac could escape and so that she could also figure out a way to escape from the flask.

"How can I be your friend? We just met," said Rico.

"No, we met before. Last time. Remember? I was running away from you with Buddy," said Karen and she was abruptly cut by Rico saying, "I knew you were assisting Buddy."

"Well, try this," she plucked out a bit of the mousse. It was sticky. She held it out to Rico. "It is delicious," she exclaimed.

"It is the same stuff," Rico said. "We CAN eat this but NOT Buddy. It is inedible for Buddy. Poor Buddy. Ha ha ha," laughed Rico. "But, I still need to make the secretion to solubilize it so that I can eat it," Rico continued. Karen looked at the plucked mousse in her hands. It was sticky.

"Look, human. We got good sensors and we know right away what food is edible and what requires secretions," explained Raymond.

"You all work so hard. You know, secreting that chemical to solubilize the mousse is a lot of work," Karen applauded them.

"Well, the mousse on the right might not require secretion. No secretion will help you save some energy. I am sorry you had to chase me. You must be so hungry," said Karen.

They all stood still around her. "You see, I float if I am left alone. That's why you saw me hold Buddy's flagellum. I mean its protruding part," explained Karen.

"But we don't have any of those parts," said Rico.

"How about if she holds on to you?" asked Raymond.

"Yeah, let's try that," Rico said. "Raymond, you are the smallest here. Now let's try to get Karen to grab on to you," Rico continued.

"OK," replied Karen.

"As long as I have my share of food too" Raymond said.

"I will make sure about that," Karen said.

Karen grabbed Raymond. It was very slimy. She kept slipping. Raymond was probably covered with slime, commonly found on the outer covering of microorganisms.

"How about if you get on top of me?" Raymond asked. Karen got on top of it and bent down and put her arms around Raymond to prevent slipping of. It was as if she was on a horse but with her arms around its body below the neck. They all went left of the mousse cave. It got brighter there because it was at the edge of the flask. Karen could see her lab from the flask's glass.

"Hmm, looks good here," Rico said. Meanwhile, Buddy and Tupac quietly swam off in the opposite direction without being caught by anyone there. Karen grabbed some of the frothy mousse and gave it to Raymond. It was greasy but not that sticky like what she got earlier.

"That looks good," Raymond said and started eating it.

"Let me show you my world," Karen said and they moved to the edge of the flask. As Karen explained the world, they kept eating and reproducing by binary fission. She made sure to take a smear of Rico's baby generation before she finally did the magic rub and was whisked out of the flask.

Chapter 5

The Quest For Understanding And Empowerment

Karen and Andy gazed out of the window at the sunset. It was autumn. The trees had reddish brown foliage. The sky was full of pink hues. And the geese were migrating to the south. There was a squirrel, nibbling on a piece of nut it was holding. Then it ran off up a tree. Karen and Andy laughed.

Inside, there was a fire burning to keep them warm.

"The sweater looks good on you," Andy said.

"Thank you. You picked the right color for the sweater. Crimson is my favorite color," Karen said.

"You're welcome," Andy replied and leaned over to give Karen a kiss and continued, "thank you for bringing me here." They loved this place, 45 minutes drive from their home. They took the day off. They went to the gym, later to bowling and then came up here for hiking. They were settled for a dinner of clam chowder and chicken potpie. That was their favorite. And how can they forget to have dark chocolate cake later on with some coffee and a fresh cinnamon stick in it.

While Karen had been hard at work in the lab, Andy had been busy with his shifts as a security guard. He had just finished off his Associate degree in Criminology. The family get-together was next weekend. It was time to give Andy a much-deserved celebration and she had brought him here. They enjoyed the band playing while they sipped their coffee, cuddled up and warm. When they got home later that evening, Andy had a surprise waiting for him. He smiled his famous smile, when he saw the gift. It was a motorbike helmet. Magenta and black. His favorite colors.

"Thank you, baby. That is very nice of you," he said, happily. They went off for a motorbike ride later on with Andy in his new helmet. They both loved motorbike rides. The air was breezy and cool and it was the perfect weather and time in the quiet night. They zoomed off.

Meanwhile in the lab, the petri plates were inoculated with the smear taken from Rico's baby generation. Also growing was a reference culture, *Mycobacterium vanbaleenii* PYR-1 for comparison with Rico.

Mycobacterium vanbaleenii PYR1

Mycobacterium vanbaleenii PYR1 was first found in the watershed of Harbor Island oil tank farm in Redfish Bay, Texas in 1986. It was notable for its ability to degrade PAHs consisting of three or more rings in their chemical structures. It is rod-shaped and non-motile. PYR stands for pyrene due to the ability of this strain to degrade pyrene and also its ability to use pyrene as an only carbon and energy source. This means that if pyrene is the only carbon and energy source in its growth culture, the strain will use it to grow.

Rico's culture was 90% related to *Mycobacterium vanbaleenii* Strain PYR1, as per DNA sequencing analyses, the same kind of analyses technique that Karen uses for identifying microorganisms, the same technique that was used in an attempt to identify Buddy. Like *Mycobacterium vanbaleenii* Strain PYR-1, Rico's culture was resistant to penicillin, the chemical produced by Alex. This chemical was analyzed using the liquid chromatography mass spectrometry after concentrating it. Alex, as Karen identified using her microorganism identification technique was a fungus, *Penicillium chrysogenum* and as the DNA sequence library comparison pointed to her, was 99.9% related to it, making its identity a sure hit, *Penicillium chrysogenum*. But Rico's culture was a mystery. Being 90% related to *Mycobacterium vanbaleenii* Strain

PYR1 and possessing some morphological and growth differences imply that Rico's culture might not be *Mycobacterium vanbaleenii* PYR1. In addition to being penicillin resistant, Rico's culture was also resistant to the other antibiotics, cephalosporin and carbapenems and so was Strain PYR-1. BUT, Rico's culture had motile cells and was twice bigger in size than *Mycobacterium vanbaleenii* Strain PYR1 which had nonmotile cells. Also, Rico's culture grew on pyrene as the only carbon and energy source in the culture thrice faster than for PYR-1. Was it a different strain of *Mycobacterium vanbaleenii*? What was it?

The use of the word strain was common in microbiology and Dr. Rogers' lab had frequently used it, more than the word subspecies.

Strain versus subspecies

A strain, by definition, is a genetic variant of a microorganism. It is an unofficial term and commonly used. For example, a flu strain. It has minor variations from the main group and might act differently in different conditions. However, the use of the term is not clear and it is fuzzy. A microorganism identified in a particular location might have the strain name attached to it, just to show that it belongs to a major genus and species, but is a bit different from others in that genus and species category.

A subspecies, on the other hand, is an official designation in taxonomy. A subspecies differs from another subspecies morphologically or in DNA sequence. The criterion for subspecies is that they should merge into a single, genetically unified population when they breed with one another. And two subspecies can breed with one another. If they can't breed due to genetic or intrinsic factors, then they are different species.

Karen observed that Rico's culture and PYR-1 cannot interbreed. *So was it a different species?* Karen thought. Karen observed the mixed culture of PYR-1 and Rico's under the real-time microscope. When grown together on pyrene, Rico's type took over the petri plate in population and PYR-1's population decreased. The new colonies were identical to Rico's type. Interesting! *So was Rico was a different species than PYR-1? Or was it a strain?*, Karen thought. Taxonomical classification often met a lot of criticism and Karen would need to do more tests, repeat the tests and consult with others to build a strong base for decision and justification. Something to think about for later.

She was worried about Buddy and Tupac and their kinds dying because of Rico. She had been adding more crude oil in the flask and for now, the growth results were stable and not decreasing. The bubbly, colorless secretion from Rico that got on her legs on the last visit gave her a little itchy rash for a few days. Chemical analyses of this chemical on the liquid chromatography mass spectrometry identified it to be a biosurfactant and strong enough to emulsify a large proportion of chemicals from crude oil. AND also kill PYR-1.

Some microorganisms produce biosurfactants to emulsify hydrophobic chemicals. It is like the action of a detergent to remove dirt when applied to clothes.

Biosurfactants

Biosurfactants are amphiphilic molecules, which means that they have both hydrophilic and hydrophobic parts in their chemical structures. Biosurfactants can help to enhance or to inhibit the removal of hydrophobic chemicals such as crude oil. They might be effective to emulsify the hydrophobic chemical, making it easier for microorganisms to break down, as with Rico and its gang. Or they might not be that effective. Even so, biosurfactants produced by one microorganism might be harmful for another one. Or they might be beneficial for others as they can be eaten as carbon and energy sources, or the emulsified hydrophobic chemical can be degraded faster by the competing microorganisms and they can grow faster compared to the ones that produce the biosurfactant. Trehalose lipid is an example of a biosurfactant produced by several Mycobacterium species.

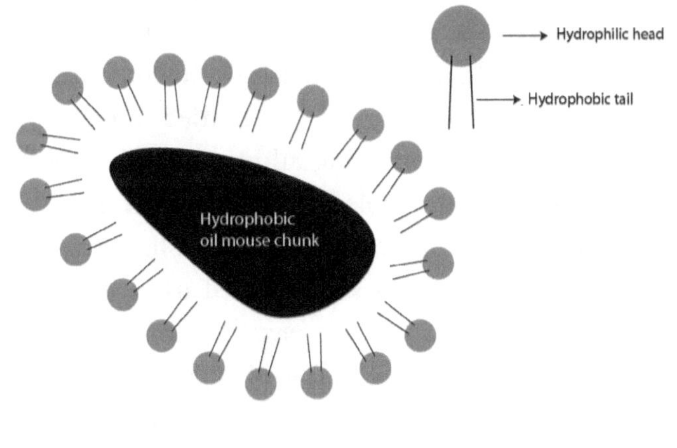

Karen found the chemical identity of this colorless, bubbly secretion from Rico using both qualitative and quantitative assays. She tried the drop collapsing test and she also tried using agar plates containing cetyltrimethyl ammonium bromide (CTAB) and methylene blue and the orcinol assay. The drop-collapsing test was basically to test if the chemical had surfactant properties. For this, she used a polystyrene Petri plate in which the well was coated with mineral oil. She put on a drop of the colorless, bubbly chemical sample she got from the flask last time. It collapsed. The theory was that anything that had low surface and interfacial tension would collapse on a surface of oil and surfactants had this property. She used emulsan, a known biosurfactant, as a positive control and water as the negative control. So this meant that the colorless, bubbly secretion from Rico was a biosurfactant, "bio" because it was produced by Rico. Next, she tried the CTAB/

methylene blue assay. For this, she prepared Petri plates containing agar supplemented with CTAB and methylene blue and crude oil. She dropped a sample of the colorless, bubbly chemical she got and observed for the formation of dark blue halos in a few minutes. When anionic biosurfactants are produced, they bind with CTAB and methylene blue. This binding leads to a color change in the medium from light blue to dark blue halos. This meant Rico produced an anionic biosurfactant.

Next, she tried the orcinol assay to measure the concentration of the biosurfactant produced from Rico. This is a colorimetric assay used to detect rhamnolipids. She acidified the bubbly, colorless sample with 1N hydrochloric acid and extracted it thrice with chloroform: methanol (2:1, v/v). The extracted supernatant was then dried and resuspended in water and to this, a solution containing sulfuric acid mixed with orcinol was added. This was heated, cooled and the optical density reading was taken at 421nm on the spectrophotometer. She extrapolated this reading in a standard curve that she prepared using another known biosurfactant called JBR 425. This gave the concentration of the biosurfactant. The reading was 10.2µg of biosurfactant per mL of sample. That was unusually high compared to biosurfactant production Karen had observed in other microorganisms in her research experience. She could have skipped the acidification and extraction part and just mixed the bubbly, colorless sample with sulfuric acid and mixed with orcinol, heated, then cooled and then taken the spectrophotometer reading. But Karen was treating the sample as if it was an unknown extract and not yet verified as a biosurfactant. In other words, she didn't want to be biased.

Karen tried methods that beside quantitation could also help her to identify the chemical nature of the biosurfactant Rico produced. She tried including TLC, HPLC-MS, FT-IR and H-NMR. It was a rhamnolipid. PYR-1 also produced a biosurfactant, a trihalose lipid. But contact with the rhamnolipid from Rico killed PYR-1!

She also tried the same tests with growth culture from Rico's and PYR-1 for quality assurance. She grew the sample and PYR-1 in fresh mineral salt medium with crude oil, the same medium Rico, Buddy and other micro-buddies grew in, using washed cells as the inoculum from a previous growth culture grown to mid-log phase as monitored by aliquot readings on the spectrophotometer. To prepare the inoculum, she washed the cells by centrifuging the culture aliquot thrice and each time re-suspending in mineral salt-only medium. The washed re-suspended cells were then used as the inoculum. At selected time intervals, aliquots were taken from this growth culture to do the biosurfactant tests- the same qualitative and quantitative tests she did with the bubbly, colorless sample. Rico's secretion was verified to be a rhamnolipid and at a maximum average amount of 11.2µg per mL of culture on day 5. That was a huge amount, again more than what Karen had ever observed in her research on biosurfactants.

She also tested the effect of the extracted biosurfactant from Rico, from the orcinol assay, on the growth of PYR-1. She added different concentrations of the extracted biosurfactant to culture flask sets containing PYR-1 in mineral salt broth and crude oil and observed the growth reading by using protein extracts of PYR-1 and the spectrophotometer. PYR-1 culture started dying within a few hours even with 0.01µg of Rico's biosurfactant per mL of culture. Wow! The biosurfactant produced by Rico and its gang was a killer! When observed under the light microscope, PYR-1 cells appeared disintegrated, just like she had seen Charlie die in the mousse cave on contact with Rico's biosurfactant.

But Rico's biosurfactant was also very effective in degrading crude oil. On day 5, with 11.2µg of Rico's biosurfactant per mL of culture, 82% of the crude oil was gone. That was the highest observed. Chemical analyses of solvent-extracted culture aliquots using the GC-MS, using the same chemical analyses techniques that Karen used for crude oil studies, showed a decrease in the concentration of the HMW-PAHs such as benzo (a)pyrene, fluoranthene and pyrene. But there was an increase in concentrations of naphthalene, and also benzoic and tricarboxylic acids. Karen had seen this kind of result before. It was called oxidative ring cleavage in which carbon bonds in the benzene rings were broken by the enzymes called oxygenases, resulting in the formation of chemicals that has less number of benzene ringed structures and are water soluble.

And the rhamnolipid produced by Rico's gang was helping them to eat these HMW-PAHS by emulsifying them.

But what was that inedible dark mousse that floated around that no one could eat, the one that Joey helped pushed toward Karen when she was with Buddy and Tupac in a oil mousse cave?? Karen analyzed it using the GC-MS. She was guessing that it would be oxidized products with double covalent bonds. And to her surprise, she was right. They were diones. Lots of them.

Diones

Diones are carbonyl covalently fused with the benzene ring structures. Benzo(a)pyrene-7,8-dione and pyrene-1,6-dione are examples. Diones can arise by oxidation and this can occur by oxygenated products produced by the metabolic processes of microorganisms. Most microorganisms couldn't break the diones down because of the double covalent bonded oxygen in the structure. Oxygen has lone pairs of electrons in this structure which can be reactive and cause damage to the enzymes around it. Diones can also undergo epoxidation and the resulting epoxide can cause DNA damage.

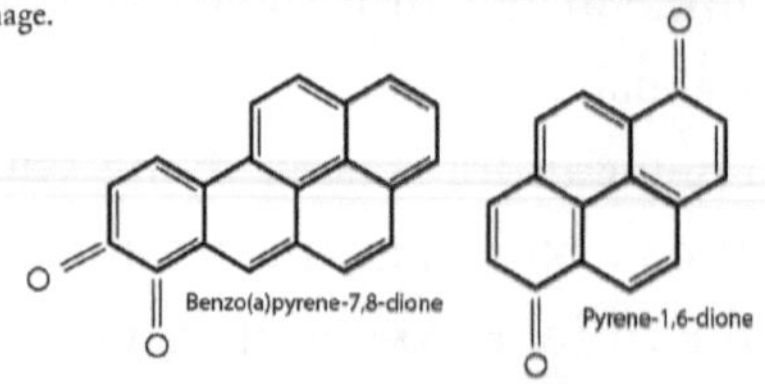

Karen identified benzo (a)pyrene-7, 8-dione and pyrene1,6-dione-products said by research to arise by autooxidation. *Can chemotaxis play a role in helping microorganisms avoid contact with diones?* Karen thought. Something to think about for future research.

Rhamnolipid from Rico was also confirmed to kill Buddy's types. She grew the sample from Buddy's gang that was confirmed by tests to be Buddy's. She took a mid-log phase inoculum of this culture grown in mineral salt medium with crude oil and then added diluted rhamnolipid from Rico, at a concentration of even with 0.01μg of Rico's biosurfactant per mL of culture. Even dilutions of this didn't stop killing Buddy's cultures. The culture started dying in a few hours. The positive control was the culture that had not received any rhamnolipid but rather a placebo of nutrients and the negative control was the uninoculated culture. Washed cells seen under the light microscope were disintegrated. Membrane broken up, lysed material. This implied that the rhamnolipid from Rico killed Buddy's culture.

Did Buddy and its gang produce any biosurfactants?, Karen thought. She ran qualitative and quantitative tests on the culture flask from Buddy's sample to detect for and measure biosurfactants. But to her surprise, all the tests were negative and implied that Buddy's gang did not produce any biosurfactant! So how was Buddy and its gang keeping alive? How were they feeding on the crude oil? She reflected back on her time in the mousse cave. She remembered seeing Tupac inside the mousse cave. Tupac had its flagellum anchored in a little hole and was feeding by endocytosis at a nearby little hole. Buddy's gang also did the same.

So the question was how was Buddy's gang surviving? What was Tupac feeding on? Could a biosurfactant produced from another friendly gang help Buddy's gang digest the HMW-PAHs in the crude oil? Maybe there was something in the surroundings around Tupac that helped him to feed in the hole in the mousse cave. Maybe a biosurfactant produced from a friendly gang nearby. Or maybe the gang produced the biosurfactant somewhere else and it was floating around, helping Tupac and others to emulsify the HMW-PAHs to feed on it. Karen remembered that she did see lots of microorganisms sticking on and budding inside the mousse cave. But she couldn't remember observing them carefully to find out if they were a different gang or part of Buddy's gang. She was focused on Tupac feeding that day.

Karen thought about the hole in the mousse. Could it be composed of LMW-PAHs? Could it be that Buddy and its gang could only feed on LMW-PAHs and did not have the means or ability to feed on HMW-PAHs due to their hydrophobicity and because they couldn't produce biosurfactants? What was the chemical composition of the hole in the mousse? What was in the hole that Tupac fed on?

She took some of the mousse from a recent flask that had the micro-buddies growing. She scooped some of the mousse out onto a glass petri plate. She dissected the portion and then scooped out the different looking locations of the mousse into different vials. There was liquid in the mousse holes and she suctioned that carefully into vials.

She extracted the samples by organic extraction and then prepared them to run on the GC-MS. The liquid in the holes were LMW-PAHS and they were also concentrated in the rims around the holes in the mousse. The rest of the mousse including the outside was mostly HMW-PAHs.

To pure, freshly set-up cultures of Buddy's gang containing mineral salt and crude oil, Karen went about doing different sets of experiments. To one set, she added benzo (a) pyrene. To another set, she added fluoranthene. To the third, she added pyrene. These were HMW-PAHs. The fourth set had phenanthrene, the fifth naphthalene and the six and seventh benzoic acid and citric acid, respectively. These were the sole carbon and energy sources and were added at 0.1% (v/v/). To another set, she added the same concentration of crude oil. She wanted to see what would happen to the oil. For the negative control she used water instead of the hydrocarbons. She put the flasks on the shaker and in the dark like she had been doing with all the other culture flasks for the micro-buddies. At selected time intervals, she took aliquots of the culture and used it for measuring the cellular protein and chemical concentration.

To her surprise, Karen noted that Buddy's gang could not digest the HMW-PAHs! She was hoping that they could maybe digest pyrene. Why was she hoping for this? No reason. Was just a thought. Maybe because *Mycobacterium vanbaleeniii* PYR-1 was a well-known microbe that could digest pyrene. And Rico could too but faster than PYR-1. Buddy's gang died in flasks that contained the HMW-PAHs. By day 4, the culture was dead. And the GC-MS analyses showed that 97% of these HMW-PAHs remained in the flask even after a week. The 2% were accounted for by diones, HMW-PAH auto-oxidation. The rest, probably photooxidized. BUT Buddy's culture could digest the LMW-PAHs and grow. In 52 hours, the culture had reached the peak in its log phase and only an average of 18% of the LMW-PAHs remained. The maximum degradation was seen for citric acid followed by benzoic acid.

However, the crude oil flask had a different story. By day 3, 98% of the HMW-PAHs were remaining while only 23% of the LMW-PAHs were left. The next day, there was 90% of the HMW-PAHs and 19% of LMW-PAHs remaining. The culture was still growing. On day 6, there was still more disappearance of the HMW-PAHs, by an average of 62%

and by day 8, this value was 31%. Meanwhile, the LMW-PAHs had increased to 45%. Yes, increased and not decreased! Then the culture started dying and there was no further reduction of HMW-PAHs. Wow! So that means that the HMW-PAHs could be eaten by Buddy's gang, even in the absence of biosurfactant production, provided that there were LMW-PAHs. One reason here could be that the enzymes that were produced to digest the LMW-PAHs could also help to digest the HMW-PAHs. The culture first eats the LMWPAHs, growing in population and concentration of the enzymes. Then they shift to eating the HMW-PAHs with the help of the enzymes, still growing more and producing more enzymes. They break down the HMW-PAHs which result in LMW-PAHs and thats why the increase in the percentage of LMW-PAHS seen on days 6 and 8. Karen thought about why they shift in food preference, from LMW-PAHs to HMWPAHs. Well, the HMW-PAHs have more carbon. More carbon bonds are broken, more energy produced. This energy is needed for their cellular functioning and growth. The culture started to die after day 8. It could be due to the depletion of micro-nutrients in the growth medium, for example the ferric chloride. Karen tested this hypothesis. There was still a bit of the culture alive on day 8. Karen added fresh trace element stock solution for mineral salt medium that contained ferric chloride. This, she added after calculating how much to add for how much medium is in the flask. The culture still continued to die. So then, she took washed cells from the culture and used that as an inoculum for a freshly prepared mineral salt medium. To this, she added the concentrations of the PAHs that were remaining on day 8, 69% of HMW-PAHs and 45% of LMW-PAHs. These comprised of the same component concentrations that she measured on day 8. The culture started growing in a few hours and first, the LMW-PAHs were degraded and in two days, the HMW-PAHs, showing the same trend in results as in the previous crude oil flask. So it was the lack of nutrients AND it could also have been the presence of dead cells. When the number of dead cells is more than live cells, it could be that chemicals produced in response to death such as some enzymes can trigger the live cells to also die quicker.

But Buddy's gang could not withstand Rico's rhamnolipid. And they were all living in one flask. Karen was opposed to the idea of removing Buddy's gang and growing in a separate flask away from Rico. It was like quarantining a human being because another human being was mean to it and killing its gang. Too sad. She had to find a way to let Buddy and its gang eat the PAHs faster like Rico and to also withstand the rhamnolipid from Rico.

Karen was familiar with synthetic surfactants. Like biosurfactants, they also helped to emulsify hydrophobic chemicals for bioremediation purpose. But unlike biosurfactants that were produced by microorganisms, synthetic surfactants, as the name implied, were manufactured. Sodium dodecyl sulfate, CTAB and Triton X100 were examples of common synthetic surfactants. Could Buddy and its gang use any of these to help eat the HMWPAHs in the mousse?

She went about answering this questions. She prepared culture flasks containing fresh mineral salt medium with crude oil and inoculated the flasks with washed cells from mid-log phase from one of the micro-buddies' flask. To one set of flasks, she added SDS. To the other, CTAB and to the third, Triton X-100. All in concentrations of 0.01% (v/v/). Karen thought to test at that concentration and if it didn't work, then she could adjust the concentrations later on with new set-ups.

She took aliquots of the culture over time and monitored them for growth, for phylogenetic analyses to see the trend on the different species- which was the same method she used to identify the different members in the culture. And she also used the aliquots for chemical analyses for the crude oil and synthetic surfactant concentration using the GC-MS.

Among the three synthetic surfactants, Triton X-100 worked! Karen looked at the results from the TRFLP technique- the same technique that she used to study the microbial population changes in the culture flasks. In two days, Buddy's gang had a population increase of 12%. Meanwhile, Rico's gang population decreased by 6% and then increased by 2% and then remained stable. SDS and CTAB killed Buddy's population and CTAB also killed Rico's population. Oh well. She looked at the *Vibrio fischerii* population. They were not affected, which was great because Karen didn't want them to be affected at all. Karen looked at the GC-MS results for the concentrations of the PAHs. There was more of the HMW-PAH degradation than without the addition of Triton X-100. In 12 hours, 38% disappearance was seen and by the end of 72 hours, 81% of it had disappeared. The LMW-PAH component at first disappeared faster, then there was a lull and then it started disappearing at a still faster rate. The culture also survived longer than without Triton X-100. The rhamnolipid production from Rico's group was at first lower but then increased and then remained steady. This was proportional to Rico's population density, i.e. when Rico's population decreased, as was seen in the beginning, then there was less of the rhamnolipid concentration compared to when the population increased.

Karen could still detect all the gangs six days later after setting the experiment. But then Buddy's gang started to die. Maybe they needed more Triton X-100 and fresh medium. She sub-cultured and used fresh medium, crude oil and 0.1% (v/v) of the Triton X-100, the same concentration of Triton X-100 that she used the first time. But this time, the results were unexpected! It didn't go as it did the first time with Triton X-100!!

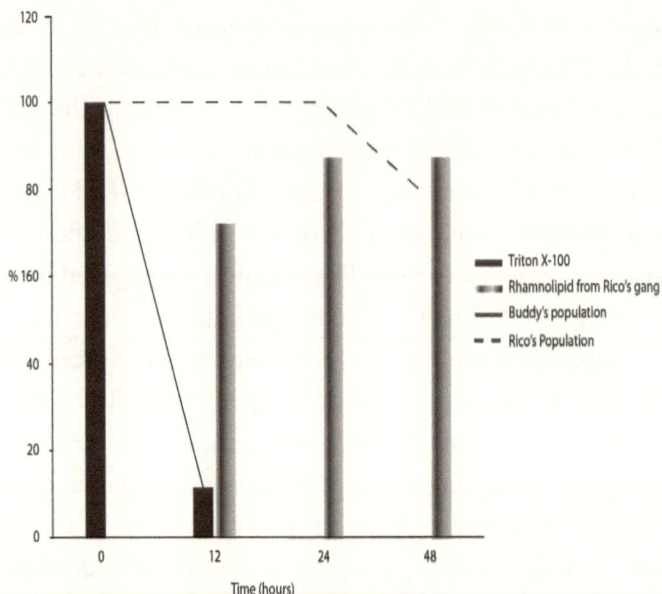

Within 12 hours, 57% of HMW-PAHs were remaining.

This value was 89% for LMW-PAHS Then in 15 hours, the

HMW-PAH degradation became stagnant while the LMWPAH degradation picked up faster.

Karen studied the two figures carefully. *When Triton X100 was gone, rhamnolipids from Rico were produced. Triton X-100 emulsified the HMW-PAHs that Rico's gang ate and deprived Buddy's gang of it. Rico's gang also probably ate the Triton X-100 too. Then, theystarted producing the rhamnolipids to help them further emulsify the HMW-PAHs,* Karen thought.

Karen tried the experiment again with 0.1% (v/v) of the Triton X-100. The same results. She tried again and again. Same results. Frustrated and not thinking, Karen dumped in 1% (v/v) of the Triton X-100 in a new flask set-up with all the other ingredients that she used before. She used mid-log phase inoculum of the microbial consortium. Buddy's population thrived! Rico's population at first decreased, then increased and remained stable. HMW-PAHs were first degraded faster than LMW-PAHs. In five hours, the concentrations of the LMW-PAHs increased and then decreased in another hour. Rico's gang started to produce rhamnolipids in 5 hours. But it didn't affect Buddy's population AS LONG AS she kept adding Triton X-100 and fresh crude oil every six hours. So she needed to keep giving fresh Triton X-100 and oil. But that was for now. What if Rico's group took control of the Triton X-100 and started eating it too this time? It didn't happen until six hours. So as long as she kept the Triton X-100 concentration steady at 1%, the population dynamic would remain constant. That means she would have to keep an eye on the flask all the time! And she had lots to do besides just monitoring the Triton X-100 concentration all the time.

What if she added more than 1% (v/v) Triton X-100? Would that affect the population? She tried the test using 2% (v/v/) with a fresh flask and all the ingredients along with the mid-log phase inoculum. The microbial population started dying right away and was undetected in a couple of hours. Karen tried 3% (v/v). To her surprise, the culture died within an hour! So 2% and 3% (v/v) of Triton X-100 was toxic to the culture.

Karen was excited to go in the flask and save Buddy's group. She made a vial of 1% (v/v) of Triton X-100. The populations in the flask containing Buddy Longtail and others were stable as she had been giving it more crude oil and ferric chloride. But she had to go in before anything new happened due to new adjustments from Rico. You never know when microorganisms can have new adjustments or if they become mutants. She looked at the time. It was 2pm and Friday. And she knew that each flask visit as per clock time lasted no more than 15 minutes. Often times, it seemed to Karen that she was in the flask for hours. Like the time they were hiding from Rico, she thought she had been in there the whole night and Andy might have been worried about her. But last time when she went in the flask, she noted the time in the back of her lab notebook before she did the magic rub and went in for a visit. And when she came out, she looked at the clock and the time in the notebook. And she had been gone only seven minutes. Karen wanted to see Buddy and its group emulsify the crude oil with Triton X-100 and she wanted to see what Rico's group would do. She had the solution of Triton X-100 in the pocket in her lab coat. She noted the time in the back of her lab notebook and then did the magic rub.

Chapter 6

We Are Buddies!

Karen watched as the 1% Triton X-100 solution emulsified the outer surface of the mousse cave. The dark black sticky material became liquidy. She observed Buddy and others take in the liquid by endocytosis. The liquid slowly vanished. Then Karen observed a colorless sac form and get expelled by exocytosis.

She thought about metabolic pathways that break down substrates. The dark, sticky material was the HMW-PAHs and they were emulsified by the Triton X-100 solution. The emulsified HMW-PAHs were then taken in by endocytosis, broken down by enzymes inside the microbes. The dark material vanished which implied that it was breaking down. The breaking down of covalent bonds in the HMW-PAH structures released energy that the microbes used in the form of ATP (adenosine triphosphate), the energy molecule in living things. The products from the breaking down were probably what the colorless secretion was. It could be HMWPAHs with less carbon rings than the starting food, LMWPAHs, sugars and water- all of this colorless.

As far as Karen knew, HMW-PAHs are oxidized with the help of oxygenases into LMW-PAHs. The oxidation process breaks open the benzene rings, which means breaking of the carbon-carbon covalent bond. When covalent bonds are broken, they release energy and this energy is stored in the form of ATP; otherwise the energy will escape and will disperse into the surroundings. So to prevent the energy from bond breaking to escape, the body stored it in the form of ATP. The benzene ring structures are split open in the oxidation process into carbon structures with less covalent bonds.

Then surprisingly, Karen saw the colorless secretion from Buddy taken in by endocytosis by Tupac.

"Yummy," Tupac said. The colorless secretion disappeared slowly in Tupac. What was that? It could be that they were feeding off each other's metabolic products. "That tasted orangey," Tupac said. Citric acid? "It helps me stay fit and strong," Tupac continued and zoomed around Karen. Karen saw Buddy take in the colorless secretion from Robby, another member of Buddy's group. Just like Buddy but bigger and quieter.

"I bet it tastes orangey too, "Karen said.

"Tart," said Buddy. "Puzzled?" Buddy asked. Karen nodded her head. "Well, you see if we eat this dark black matter, then we produce orangey-tasting secretion. If we eat this light black matter, then we produce tangy-tasting secretion. So depending on what we eat, we produce different types of secretion. And then we share what we produce. Some of us like to eat the orangey secretion and some of us, the tangy. And then there is an lemony-tasting secretion. There are so many of it and we ALL SHARE what we produce."

"But you can't see the secretions or smell them. How do you pick what you want to eat?" asked Karen.

"We can chemically detect the secretions. Don't ask me how. I don't know. All I know is that our juices start churning and lead us to what we prefer to eat," Buddy explained.

"Hey Tupac, I thought you were going to make that tangy stuff, not this sour stuff by eating this light black material," Buddy said.

"Fooled you," Tupac laughed.

"Last time, you made that tangy stuff, that was good. But this sour stuff, why?" Buddy asked.

"I can do what I want with this light black stuff. It takes me more energy to make that tangy stuff. So I made this sour stuff this time," explained Tupac. So this implied that Buddy's gang were capable of multiple, alternative pathways using the same substrate and that they were capable of ingesting different substrates too using the help of

Triton X100 solution to emulsify the hydrophobic substrate. Interesting. What pathway to use depended on how much energy they had left and enzymes produced.

"Let's go, Karen," Buddy said. They were around the mousse cave with light from Bernie's gang. Everyone started scattering. Karen could see Rico's gang swarm moving towards them.

"No… wait, they can't harm you this time," Karen said, remembering the laboratory tests she did with 1% Triton X100 solution. Rico's gang fed on the Triton X-100 emulsified HMW-PAHs. And it didn't produce rhamnolipids. But for until five hours. She wanted to see what would happen to both gangs when they were in the presence of the 1% Triton X-100 solution. She had two more vials each of the 1% Triton X-100 solution and crude oil in her pocket, just in case she would need more to help Buddy's gang It didn't need to be diluted if she stays in the flask for less than an hour.

Rico's gang got closer. Tupac, Robby and others from the group went into hiding in the cave. Buddy was there with Karen was holding onto its flagellum. Bernie and its gang were there too. After all, they didn't need to run from Rico or anyone. They were friendly and fed on decomposed, dead bodies. The yellow rod shapes of Rico and the gang became clear.

"Hoolah!" Rico said, seeming very happy. "What's up, my lady? I see that you still have both legs. So my poison didn't kill you, huh?" Rico said, circling Karen. "Hey, my little wimp. Not scared of me this time, are you?" Rico continued, circling Buddy now. Karen looked at Buddy and Buddy was quiet and still. "Where is that little baby of yours?" Rico asked and then went to the cave. "Tupac, yohooo, hey sweet Tupaaac," it said.

"What?" came Tupac's squeaky voice.

"Come on out here," Rico said and went in deeper. The openings in the cave were very narrow but Karen saw that Rico could squeeze in its body. That's because the membrane covering is fluidy. It is made of phospholipids and they are present like heads and tails aligned next to each other and every once in a while, the phospholipids can flip-flop or exchange places with their neighbor phospholipids. The bent tails of the phospholipids prevent them from packing together and this also helps in membrane fluidity. The presence of some molecules such as cholesterol and also temperature can reduce phospholipid movement. This fluid membrane theory also holds for membranes found in other cells. Rico's rod shaped body became long and it squeezed into a hole. Karen saw Tupac come out from another hole out of the mousse cave and flee away quietly.

"Shhhh," Buddy said. Poor Tupac. How naive was it, announcing its presence to Rico.

"I am here," Tupac replied. It was behind Buddy and Karen.

"TUPAC!" Rico roared and swiftly came out of the cave. Before Rico and Tupac got into a chase game, Karen called out, "Alright everyone. I have a treat for you all. I have a treat for you too, Rico." Rico and its gang surrounded Karen.

"Ready?" Karen asked.

"Yeah, come on, where is the treat?" Rico asked restlessly.

"Calm down, will you?" Karen said.

"For what? We got to eat all this mousse before it spoils or someone else gets it. Where is the treat?" Rico asked.

"Buddy, you ready?" Karen asked.

"Yeah," Buddy replied.

Karen took out a vial of Triton X-100 solution. All the micro-buddies moved down and up as per the motion of Karen's hand holding the vial. She only had one free hand and her other hand was holding Buddy's flagellum. As soon as she moved the glass vial to her mouth to twist loosen the cap, Tupac stared wailing.

"Don't poison yourself, Karen, we will die if you do," whimpered Tupac.

"She is fooling us," roared Rico.

"Hey, hey, let me tell you," Karen retorted, waving her hand with the vial in it to get attention and to prevent a fight.

"Let the poor thing talk," Carrie said.

"Poor thing, talk," Rico said in a rebuking tone. "Come on Rico, behave yourself," Buddy said.

"Or else what? Get killed by me?" Rico said and the gang started laughing.

"We are going to die," Tupac whimpered. It sounded like sixth grade to Karen. Refreshing in some ways from the quiet life she led but also irritating right now.

"OK, OK, everyone listen. No one will die," Karen said.

"But she is going to die by eating that vial she put on her mouth," Rico said and its gang started laughing. "No, no, I am not going to eat the vial. I need to open it and spill it so that you can see the magic. And to open it, I need to put it on my mouth. I only have one hand and I can't open this with one hand. So I will use my mouth," Karen explained. She quickly put it on her mouth, grasped the lid with her teeth and twisted it open. Then she opened the lid with her free hand and spilled some of the liquid from it on the mousse. The dark black material from the mousse started swimming. It was like taking paint off from the wall.

"That's yummy," Rico said and started feeding on the emulsified black material from the mousse by endocytosis. There was a lot of the Triton X-100 solution all around.

"Come on, Buddy, Tupac, everyone, there is a lot for everyone," Karen said. All the micro-buddies except for Bernie's gang ran over. Bernie's gang fed on decomposing material and didn't eat emulsified PAHs. Karen realized that she was holding Buddy's flagellum and so maybe that's why Buddy didn't run over.

"Hey, Carrie, can I hold onto you while Buddy goes off to feed?" Karen asked. Carrie came over and Karen held onto Carrie's polar flagella. Buddy swam over and starting eating the emulsified material by endocytosis.

"Thank you, Karen," Buddy said. "Bernie, make sure to be around her or she will slip."

"Joey, Harry, Beanie, come on gang," Bernie said. "Beanie's not here," Joey replied.

"Never mind. You come over, Joey," Bernie replied. Beanie always stayed and fed on dead bodies in the caves. Carrie's flagella were slimy and yes, hard to keep a grip on, but the gang members around her acted like a wall to prevent her from slipping. Karen saw Buddy's and Rico's gangs ingest the emulsified black material by endocytosis. She also saw something exciting!

The different gangs were producing different sized and colored secretions after eating the emulsified black material. The secretions came out by exocytosis. Might be different metabolic pathways operating in different groups and producing different intermediates and end products, Karen thought. There were some known pathways for different components of the crude oil by different organisms. For example, *Mycobacterium sp.* strain PYR-1 can degrade pyrene by the Kiyohara and the o-phthalate pathway. Another *Mycobacterium sp.*, strain RJG II-135 can degrade pyrene by the upper pathway while *Sphingomonas paucimobolis* strain EPA 505 can degrade pyrene by the lower pathway.

At first, both Rico's and Buddy's gang were feeding on the Triton X-100 solution emulsified material and produced different secretions that were eaten by each other. Karen looked more carefully. One secretion bubble was being avoided by Rico's gang. Those that came in contact died! This secretion was produced by Buddy's gang and Rico's gang avoided it or they died. That explained why Rico's population declined in the beginning with 1% (v/v) Triton X-100. This was produced when Buddy's gang ate a greyish looking part of the emulsified mousse. But this was not present too much. Soon, there was no more of this greyish looking emulsified mousse and so no more of the killer secretion from Buddy. Rico's gang stopped being killed.

Karen decided to go out of the flask and return in six hours and then seven and eight hours later.

SIX HOURS LATER (7 PM, FRIDAY)

The concentrations of the HMW-PAHs were decreasing as the mousse had become chunks. Rico's gang were producing rhamnolipids to eat the blackish, tarry-looking remains of the mousse. On eating this, they produced yellowish secretions and Buddy's gang started eating it. Karen observed very carefully. Some of Rico's gang were also were eating the LMW-PAHS by endocytosis and were producing white secretions by exocytosis that were then taken in by Buddy's gang by endocytosis.

Buddy's gang didn't eat any LMW-PAHs. They relied completely on the yellowish and whitish material produced by Rico's gang and bloomed in population. They avoided contact with the rhamnolipid. That's how Buddy's population stayed high all the time!

ONE HOUR LATER (8 PM, FRIDAY)

The caves and the liquid in the mousse were mostly gone. Rico kept producing rhamnolipids. And this time, there was no more of the yellowish and whitish secretions from Rico. Buddy's gang started dying. Karen had to pour in more oil mousse and 1% (v/v) of the Triton X-100. She observed the same thing she did when she poured the last vial.

Suddenly, Karen saw something startling. A tan, rodshaped microbuddy with one flagellum moving around in front of her. The flagellum didn't propel as it did in living micro-buddies. But the body wasn't disintegrated either. Karen looked more carefully at it. It had two "turfs" coming out from most places on its body. It was Buddy!

"No!" Karen yelled. She let go of Bernie's flagellum but was surrounded by Bernie's gang and she couldn't get through to Buddy. "Let me go. Someone please help Buddy!" she yelled.

"No one can help the old Buddy. It is dead now! Have fun with the new Buddy," Rico said and started laughing.

"But your population is flourishing. And I just gave you some of that magic chemical I have been giving you every six hours. It is called Triton X-100. How can Buddy die?" Karen started wailing.

Karen pushed by the others and tried to swim to Buddy. But she floated off. She tried the swim movement again to propel forward. But no, she floated off. It was weightlessness, as if she was on the moon. But she wasn't on the moon. She was in the flask and her friend, Buddy, had just died. Her best friend. Her micro-buddy who made her life happier and easier and more meaningful. She started sobbing. She felt empty. She didn't know what to do with herself. She kept kicking but she drifted off into nowhere, pure blackness. She remembered Buddy's voice, so manly. It was Buddy who introduced her to the flask, Buddy who guided her to the world in the flask, Buddy who was with her all the time in the flask, so protective, so supportive, and so guiding. And now it was all disintegrated. And she couldn't do anything to save its life. She was sobbing hard and crumpled up, and floating into nowhere.

"We can't let her go. The chemical will irritate her," Carrie said. By now, Buddy's body was being disintegrated.

Karen felt something rubbing against her. There was a lot of rubbing, gentle tender rubbing on her back and a soft voice. "It is alright Karen. It is OK." It was Carrie. "We all die and we reproduce," Carrie said. Karen hugged Carrie's slimy flagella. Bernie, Carrie and Joey were all around her. And so was Tupac who kept rubbing her back gently.

"Cheer up, Karen. Buddy will grow up soon and then it will take you around," Tupac said.

Karen looked up and said, "Buddy is dead, Tupac." Then it occurred to her about what Carrie had said- about reproduction- bacteria reproduce by binary fission. Just like Karen observed Charlie do. One split into two, two into four and so on and each of the offspring are just like the parents unless of course there is some shuffling or mutation in the genes due to replication of material during binary fission.

Karen had been coming to the flask so often…almost three months now. How could Buddy and others still be the same old Buddy and others? Bacteria reproduce in seconds and the old ones die. So, the Buddy she had been meeting was the new Buddy who grew up and acted like the old Buddy? Same for Tupac and the others? Karen felt weird. But it was the fact. The increasing population that she saw for Buddy's gang by adding 1% Triton X-100 (v/v/) implied higher binary fission than death per unit time. That's how population increase. There is not a population where there is no death and more new lives.

"The legacy lives on, Karen. There will always be Buddy and there will always be all of us. We might get old and die but our progeny live and continue our legacy," Carrie explained. Karen had stopped crying and was still holding onto Carrie's flagella.

"So there is little Buddy?" Karen asked.

"Oh yeah! It is growing up. It is a Buddy clone just as all our generations are our clones. Soon it will take you for a ride," Tupac said excitedly and lashed its flagellum. "Here it comes," Tupac yelled excitedly. Karen saw a small, tan, round organism with one flagellum swim towards them.

"Howdy, guys!" it said. It sounded just like Buddy. Karen was bewildered.

"Hey Buddy," they all replied in unison.

"Hey Karen," Buddy said. Karen didn't know what to say. She was still in shock. So every time she came into the flask, she was met with a new generation Buddy. How can she not realize that until now?

"Karen is shy of you, Buddy," Tupac squeaked. "Very shy," Tupac whispered.

Karen felt stupid and said, " I am not shy."

"She was crying. Boo hoo hoo. Like a hyena," Tupac said and they all started laughing.

"Why was she crying?" Buddy asked.

"Because you died," Tupac replied.

"Nonsense. We all die and we all leave babies that grow up like us," replied Buddy.

That's right and that's what I told her," Carrie said.

"Care for a ride?" Buddy asked her and extended its flagellum to her. Just like the old Buddy. By this time, Buddy had grown up to the size of the old Buddy and there was no telling it from the old Buddy. Karen held onto its flagellum and they all went off in the mousy world.

"Ha ha ha," Karen heard a chortled laugh from Rico. "So, you found Buddy! Ha ha ha," Rico continued and kept producing the rhamnolipid and eating the black mousse. "You should have been a bacterium, Karen. Then you would be in forever with Buddy. The way you cried, ooh ha ha ha ha," Rico continued. "So new Buddy, you got all your parts or was something missing while you were formed from old Buddy?" Rico asked. Buddy, Tupac and Bernie's gang were all around Karen.

Karen was still emotional to know that old Buddy died. Who knows how many Buddys had died and how many new ones were with her all this time in her visits to the flask. She was enraged at Rico's attitude. Rico didn't seem to have any regard for life or death. Of course many Ricos died and many new ones formed and who knew which Rico from which generation was here now. But Karen was enraged at the way Rico talked and that it produced the deadly rhamnolipid that kept Buddy's group away from it and the edible mousse.

She wanted to scare Rico for once. Just to scare it. She was enraged Rico's attitude. Suddenly, she took out the 3% (v/v/) vial of Triton X-100 solution. Last time when she got into the flask, she realized that she grabbed the wrong extra vial of Triton X-100. This concentration, as Karen had tested in the lab, killed the entire culture. She didn't want to kill Buddy's group or any other group. But she wanted to kill Rico. See it die… She twisted opened the lid with her mouth and then swung the open vial in front of Rico.

"Run, Buddy, Tupac, go, this will kill," she yelled and let go of Buddy's flagellum. Buddy kept giving Karen its flagellum.

"Hold on to it, Karen," it said. But Karen would have none of it. "No Buddy. No. Run. Don't let the solution get you. This will kill you," Karen said. But Buddy would have none of it and Karen yelled, "go away, Buddy. Please. I will hold onto Carrie," Karen said and saw Carrie nearby. She grabbed Carrie's flagella. But then she saw the unexpected. The 3% (v/v) Triton X-100 solution touched Carrie. Carrie was being disintegrated. Rico and its gang had already run off. They were nowhere in sight.

"Here, Karen. Hold onto this," Buddy said softly. Karen grabbed Buddy's flagellum. She was terrified. Carrie's membrane was melting off and it was being disintegrated. She started crying.

"Run, everyone run," Buddy yelled and took off with Karen. They glided away from the spill place. Karen was sobbing. How stupid could she be? Now Carrie was dead. Her friend. She just never thought of it. Carrie's group was providing her with light so that she could see in the dark. And she never thought that it could die because Carrie's group stayed alive in contact with the rhamnolipid from Rico. But how could she forget that nothing, just nothing, would stay alive with 3% (v/v/) of the Triton X-100 solution? How could she forget that? And the gang that provided her with light just so she could see and understand the world in the flask had a member killed. She asked to hold onto Carrie's flagella and Carrie obliged without any care for its life.

"Karen, look at Tupac," Buddy said. Karen was sobbing and didn't want to look up. She was very hurt at Carrie's death.

"Look at me, will you?" Tupac asked and lashed its flagellum at Karen's face. Slimy and soily smelling. But still, Karen kept sobbing and didn't respond. Tupac inserted its flagellum in Karen's ear and tickled.

"Stop it," Karen said.

"No, you have to look up," Tupac said and tickled her ears again.

"Hey Karen," a voice said. It sounded like Carrie. Karen looked up. There was Tupac in front of her and pointed to an organism with its flagellum. It was Carrie! Carrie had longer polar flagella than the rest of the gang. It had a bright light like Bernie and had a smooth appearance. But it looked a bit smaller than the old Carrie. Maybe it will grow up to the same size soon, Karen thought.

"Carrie?" she said.

"Yeah, it is me, Carrie. What are you crying about, big girl?" Carrie asked.

"Just nothing. I am so stupid," Karen said.

"No you are not. Don't say that. You are a living thing, just like us. And all living things make mistakes," Carrie said. "If you were perfect, then you would be a nonliving thing," Carrie said. By now, Carrie had grown to the same full size as the old Carrie. Karen hugged Carrie's flagella. "By now, remember Karen. We all die but we reproduce and leave behind our clones," Carrie said.

"Is Karen a clone?" Tupac asked. All the groups were around Karen.

"Are you a clone?" Buddy asked. Karen laughed. "No, I am not a clone," she said.

"Then how do you reproduce?" Carrie asked. Karen blushed. The groups were still around her and there was silence. That was embarrassing.

"Yeah, how do you reproduce?" Buddy asked.

"We mate and produce an embryo that grows up into a human," she said.

"Mate?" Buddy asked. "How?"

"Look, we make babies but not like how you do it. It is just different. And no, our babies are not clones. The reason you are clones is because your offspring get the exact same copy of everything, including your chromosomes. Our babies get one half of the chromosomes from the mom and one half from the dad and they mix up and produce a baby that is different in appearance from the mom and dad," she explained. There was silence and then Buddy asked, "what are chromosomes?"

"Chromosomes are these long strands that contain genetic materials," she answered and then looked to see if she could locate them in Buddy. She saw them. "See this, these are chromosomes," she said, pointing to the long strands in Buddy.

"And I thought they were zebra strips," Tupac said and they all started laughing.

They glided through the mousse caves, with Karen holding Buddy's flagellum.

"Hey guys," came a group's voice.

"That's Rico's gang," Tupac said wearily.

"Don't worry, ignore them," Buddy said and kept gliding.

"But I am hungry," Tupac wailed.

"But you know that if you go there, that poison from the group will be there and you will die," Buddy said.

"I will go in the cave," Tupac said.

"No wait, Tupac," Karen said. "Look guys, I will get out of the flask and add some water. If that doesn't help, I will sub-culture you. I got to. Or this spreading 3% (v/v) Triton X-100 will kill you all. I will also give you food. Take me out. I will come back, promise!"

"But what if you forget?" asked Buddy.

"I will not. After all, we are friends and will always look out for each other," Karen said. They all cheered around Karen as she got whisked out of the flask.

Diluting the medium in the water did help initially. But then the population started to decrease. So Karen had to subculture. The populations were happy and thriving with continuous addition of 1% (v/v) Triton X-100 and fresh crude oil. "Stay healthy and happy, micro-buddies," she said, peering at the flask. All was going well in the micro-buddies world and she made many trips. And often so, she wished she stayed behind in the flask with the micro-buddies.

A month later, Andy had proposed to her and they were getting married during the Christmas break. Her research manuscript on crude oil degradation using Triton X-100 solution had been accepted and she had also received research funds on that topic to carry out a field study for an oil company. Her Master's thesis had been moving very smoothly with insightful information and she would be defending it next spring. All this because of the microbuddies. Being able to go in the flask and interact in that world had allowed her to have a deeper understanding of the microbial world and about life in general. The timer beeped. It was 3 pm, time for her meeting with Dr. Rogers. She put away the flask on the incubator in the dark and set the speed.

"So long micro-buddies, see you guys soon. Love you," she said and ran off.